I0564069

THE BOOK OF ABRASAX

THE BOOK OF ABRASAX

A Grimoire of the Hidden Gods

Michael Cecchetelli

Nephilim Press
2012

The Book of Abrasax

Copyright © 2014 Nephilim Press
ISBN: 978-0-9905687-2-8
1st Paperback Edition

All rights reserved. No part of this book may be used or reproduced in any manner whatsoever, including electronically, without written permission from the author except in the case of brief quotations embodied in critical articles and reviews.

He who knows, and knows that he knows, is a wise man,

Listen to him!

He who knows, and does not know that he knows, is asleep,

Awaken him!

He who does not know, and knows that he does not know, Wants to learn...

Teach him!

He who does not know, and does not know that he does not know, Is a fool...

Shun him!

DEDICATION

As always, my work is dedicated to

My Father

Silvia Martinez, My Nefertari

Gratias Vobis Ago:

To HE.

To my brothers, Trece, Indio, A-Shot and Chino,
The Kings Among Kings...

Eladio "Arcangel" Castro,
May he Rest In Peace in the Bosom of
The Almighty Father, King of Kings

Gustavo "Lord Gino" Colon,
Augustin "King Tino" Zambrano, and
Alex "Grim" Delgado, buried for eternity in
the belly of the beast that is the Bureau of Prisons

AMOR DE REY

The Author Wishes To Extend His Thanks to The Following

Jason "Inominandum" Miller –
For his excellent contribution to this work
and his continued friendship

Derik Richards
My editor and friend for managing to
correct my millions of punctuation errors
whilst refraining from pulling out his hair

Frater Rufus Opus
For having supported me from the
beginning and opened my eyes to a world of possibilities

Asterion
For his masterful illustration of this volume

Christopher "Frater AIT" Bradford
For his brotherhood and work in bringing life
to a terminally ill web presence

Peter and Alkistis at Scarlet Imprint, Erzebet and Dis at Hadean
and Jim Banner at Trident
For their continued support and for
having believed in me from the beginning

Marilyn and Keith at Weiser Antiquarian Books
For their friendship, generosity and wise counsel

Jonathan Davies at Midian Books
Also for his continued friendship and help
in finding long sought after volumes I'd given up hope on owning.

AND, OF COURSE...

Frank Redd at Nephilim Press
For sharing my vision for the present work, and giving me the
creative license to bring it to life in exactly the manner I envisioned.

CONTENTS

INTRODUCTION

W ITHIN THE WALLS of academia there exists a corpus of magickal praxis predating the Renaissance and classical grimoires by centuries, which has heretofore only been examined by those whose interests lie purely in the historical and scholastic arenas. Like the Greek Magical Papyri (*Papyri Graecae Magicae* or "PGM") – which constitutes one portion of this corpus – these texts are a highly syncretic union of Egyptian, Greek, Persian, Coptic Christian, and Gnostic magickal praxis. The techniques within seamlessly fuse ἐπαοιδαί, or incantations, with γοητείαι, their form of witchcraft, and spells, or θέλξεις.

In this way, integrating adjuration of the traditional Judeo-Christian-inspired angelic hierarchies with invocation of Graeco-Egyptian deities and methods that would, in our present era, be viewed as closely resembling Hoodoo practices, these Coptic Egyptian magicians developed a comprehensive system of magick. The magickal work we find in this corpus illuminates both the immediately practical and the transcendentally spiritual – offering some of the earliest methods of achieving necessary material or tangible change in one's life, such as protection from disease, as well as those techniques with which I am primarily concerned: rites of evocation and invocation.

Despite the immediately evident value of this material to the practicing magician, it has gone unnoticed by all but myself and perhaps a handful of others who have happened upon it in one form or another. With the present volume, I propose to change that and to bring into prominence an entire lineage of magickal practice that has, until now, evaded serious attention. In addition to bringing forth the techniques of this most ancient system for those among you who will undoubtedly make use thereof in your own work,

I also hope to inspire others to begin seeking further sources for examples of this system and its derivations.

My own introduction to this underexplored field of magick came by way of one of the aforementioned academic texts. During my research into the provenance of another grimoiric manuscript on which I planned to work, I came upon a scholarly paper in which some of the same names of power were also found. After reading the first several chapters I was immediately intrigued and moved to abandon the project on which I was working – a volume that would have contained a few of the Faustian grimoires which were at that time unpublished or underpublished – in favor of focusing on a study of the magicks of the Coptic Egyptians.

For the better part of two years, I spent whatever time I could in research, development, and experimentation with the system of magick found herein, and have continued its evolution in the years that have passed since then. Because the corpus from which I've drawn the rites contained in this volume is far more vast than anything I could present in one, two, or even three books, I have endeavored to bring you what I consider to be the best and most effective examples of both the practical and transcendental magicks for this tome. I have myself made use of most of what you will find within, and what I haven't used, my students have – some of which I have discussed on my blog or in previous books to which I have contributed. All things considered, I have found the workings presented here to be of great avail, having achieved with them results equaling, even surpassing at times, those from my grimoiric work.

Another aspect of the magick I've drawn from this corpus which I hold of great value is the adaptability and flexibility of its rites. One example of this is the rite I previously summarized on my blog and in subsequent releases, which I have used successfully as a protective rite, as an exorcism, and as an invocation. The rite of which I speak may be found herein, of course.

It is my desire to formulate this book as did the fathers of the grimoires with their classics: light on theory and heavy on praxis. To that end, I am foregoing much of the "why" in favor of presenting a large amount of "how," and allowing the magick contained in this book to stand on its own; hopefully , by omitting any theories I've developed over the course of my studies, I will provoke discussion and dissection by those whose interest is as piqued as my was my own.

Despite this, I find it behooves me to touch briefly in this introduction on the origins of this magickal corpus: from whence it comes to us and from what period of time, how it was recorded and preserved, who were the likely practitioners, and who are the deities upon which they called. Those who are disinterested in the historical background of this work are welcome to skip ahead to the grimoire proper, as I myself am more often than not wont to do.

Origins

With few exceptions, the magick contained herein is drawn from codices and scrolls of Coptic Egypt, dating as far back as 100 CE and as late as the 11th century. The Greek Magical Papyri (PGM), with which the reader may be well-acquainted, represents a significant portion of this corpus, however the system itself is much more than just the PGM. The most widely available translation of the PGM with which most are familiar, that of Hans Dieter Betz, is in fact only a piece of a much larger puzzle, as Betz admittedly kept all of the overtly Christian portions out of his book. While Betz' omission of those rites which were Christian in tone does little to take away from the immense value of his work, it is a disservice to those such as myself whose interest in these papyri is their practical application. For this reason, while I will here present material like unto that in Betz' PGM (that is to say, devoid of Judeo-Christian influences), I have strived to dedicate the bulk of this volume to those rites Betz excluded.

While I am rather outspoken in my condemnation of all things Catholic, as well as many of the mainstream Christian sects, this magickal system should not be associated with these hypocritical groups, for it bears no resemblance to anything of theirs. It is, in stark contrast, a representation of the true Christianity and the true teachings of the Master Yehshua, as known to the Coptic Egyptians.

We also find Roman and Egyptian influences, and to a lesser extent, traces of Solomonic Magick. Represented well in these works are the "Gnostic" texts as discovered in Nag Hammadi, including the angelology to be found in that library. The source materials for the many academic works in which these texts are contained include pottery sheds, wooden and limestone tablets, and fragments of papyrus and early forms of paper common to Egypt during this period, as with the PGM, these have many illegible, missing, or unintelligible sections which academia has been unable to restore but which I endeavor here to present in as complete and usable a form as possible.

Present throughout these works are innumerable "words of power" or *voces magicae*, and divine names, some with which the reader will be familiar, such as IAO[1] and Sabaoth[2], and some which are less recognizable such as Ialdabaoth[3] and Marmaraōth[4], which are also to be found in the PGM. Also used are some names for which derivation or explanation eludes me, despite my best efforts to source them.

Although making use of both lesser known and, as far as I can discern, original words of power, the aspirations of the first practitioners of this magick resemble those of much later works in that they focus mainly on protection, procurement of love or sex, healing, cursing, and obtaining of wisdom and establishment of contact with divine beings. Indeed, while the methodology of the magus throughout history has changed substantially, it seems that these primary goals remain constant, bridging the gap between the eldest and most modern of traditions.

In this volume we will explore what I consider the most useful examples, at least in my own experience, of each of these categories of workings:

- Securing of Space – that is to say, those rites whose purpose resembles those of the more widely known "banishing" rites

- Amorous Magick – rites whose goal is to attract, secure, or protect love, sex, and intimacy

- Wealth and Prosperity – those workings the intent of which is to attract prosperity or fortune

- Rites of Protection – workings designed to protect the practitioner and/or those for whom he works from the world's perils and ills

- Curses and Attack Magick – magickal rites designed to bring harm to another

- Transcendent Magicks – Invocation and evocation proper, initiation and empowerment

---

1 ΙΑΦ
2 ϹΑΒΑΦΤ
3 ΑΒΡΑΧΑϹ
4 ΜΑΡΜΑΡΑΦΥ

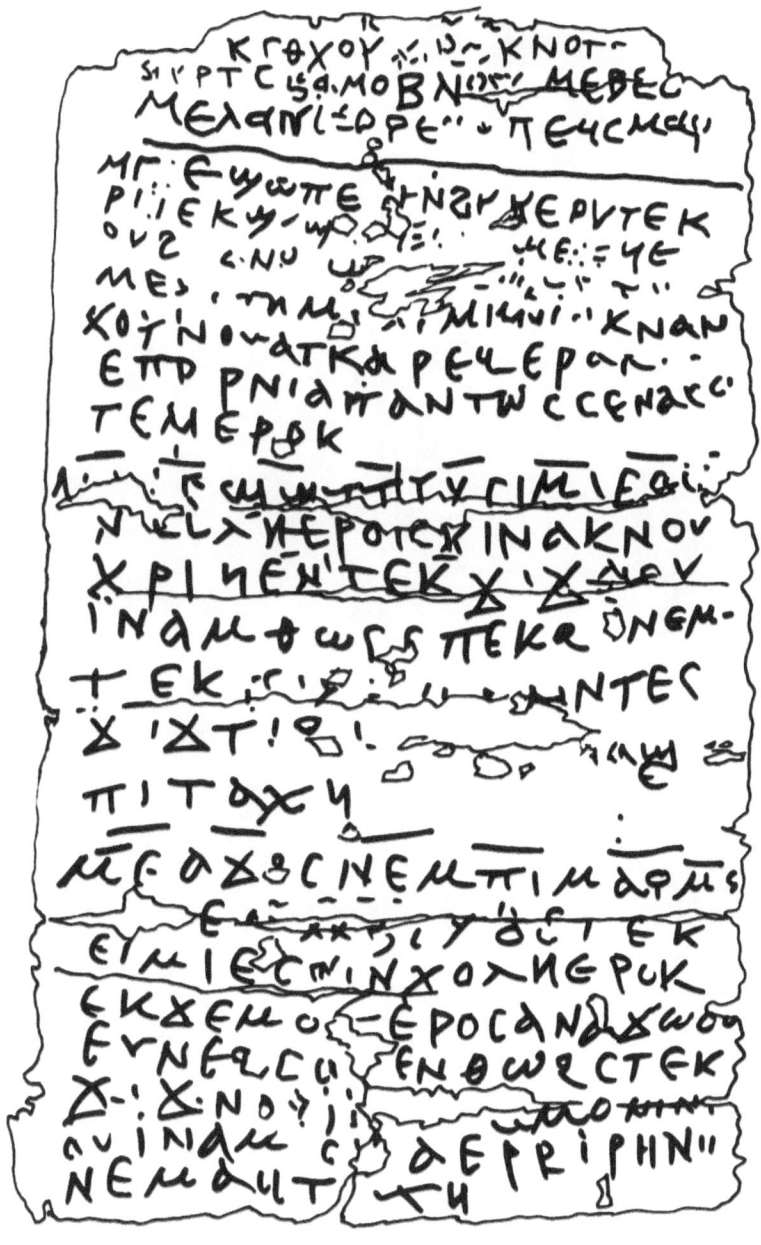

An example of the papyri of this corpus

PREFACE

Before proceeding to the corpus of this work it behooves me to make the following disclaimer. This is not a book for those whose interest in magick lies purely in the anthropological and academic studies thereof.

While I hold such individuals in very high regard, and am eternally grateful to men like Joe Peterson and Dan Harms who, through their exacting, precise, and meticulously researched critical versions of our classics, have made at least as large a contribution to the grimoire tradition as we practitioners I must realistically acknowledge that this is likely not a work in which they will find much value. This is simply because this text is being presented as a modern grimoire – that is to say a working magus' book of magick. While every effort has been made to remain as true to the original texts as possible, my interest in these works is not academic but rather practical; I have thus taken certain liberties in correcting portions of the papyri which are indiscernible in order to restore the magickal practices therein.

Before the reader begins to fret and become concerned that the rites contained in this book may be bastardized versions of the originals or unfaithful constructs of my own design, let me put your mind at ease by explaining the liberties to which I refer.

In the papyri from which these rites are drawn, among the words of power used we find the names "AKRAMACHARI," "AGRAMMACHAMARI," "AGRAMAKARI" and several other variants which are all corruptions of ΑΓΡΑΜΜΑϨΑΜΑΡΙ. While the academic approach would be to present these words precisely as they are found in the papyri to preserve the accuracy of the translation, as a practicing magus whose interest is in reproducing the results obtained by the originators, I replace these numerous spellings with "AKRAMMACHAMARI." Likewise, where we find "ABLATHANALBA,"

"ABTHALANABLA," et. al., I have replaced all such variations with ABLA-NATHANALBA, the correct way to express ΑΒΛΑΝΑΥΑΝΑΛΒΑ, a palindrome for which we have no translation and yet one of immense power.

Another such liberty has been to restore missing sections of incantations with identical sections from elsewhere in the corpus. An example is when, in one rite, we find the following:

In the name of Michael, the Peace
Of Gabriel, the Grace
Raphael, the Power
Suriel, the Will
Rag... [Missing Fragment]

Here the academician correctly denotes the missing fragment of text by placing brackets where they belong and moves on to the next discernible section. Since my own interest lies not in the precision of the transcription but the efficacy of the magick therein, I look elsewhere in the papyri and find, in a rite of similar intent,

In the name of Michael, the Peace
Of Gabriel, the Grace
Raphael, the Power
Suriel, the Will
Raguel, the Truth
Anael, the Glory
By Seraphuel, the Doctoring and Healing...

And restore the prior rite using the text of the latter.

Therefore while I have the utmost respect for those who commit endless time, effort, and resources to the academic study of these ancient texts of magick – and am truly grateful for all that they have done to further the western magickal tradition – I must warn that this volume does not conform to the standards to which they hold themselves scholastically.

To the practicing magus, however, I am pleased to introduce what I am certain will be a body of work of great use to you.

THE CORONASTRUM

Before we move forward to the Grimoire proper, I am obliged to introduce the reader to a "sign" which he will use throughout his work with the system of magick that follows. The sign of which I speak, – although I use the term loosely as I find it altogether inadequate in expression of that which you will learn momentarily – is used in much the same way the Golden Dawn and its offshoots use the Signs of the Enterer, of Silence, of Osiris Risen, and the like. Upon use of this sign, the magus will find it to be of great magickal potency in and of itself.

The gesture I am now to introduce has never before been published. It is unknown to all extant magickal orders and has never before been used outside my own brotherhood and circle, into whose weekly adorations and prayers I interjected it. It is, nonetheless, of greater power than any such "sign" of which I have ever known.

Such lofty claims as these will undoubtedly draw the ire of many who have devoted more of their lives to practical magick than I, and who have spent decades more than I have lived in study of the traditions which make frequent use of the aforementioned signs. Despite this, I am quite confident that in a brief moment when this sign is demonstrated publicly for the first time ever, even a passing glance will serve to assure the most skeptical among you of its value, for it will be at once recognized.

Yet before introducing the gesture proper, it is fitting to offer some insight for those of my readers who are unfamiliar with the signs mentioned above (those of the Enterer, Osiris Slain, the Sign of Apophis and Typhon, etc.) and as to how such hand gestures and signs bear relevance to grimoiric magick. While anyone whose path has at some point intersected with Golden Dawn traditional ritual magick, or even via Crowley in his signs of N.O.X., Hoor Paar Krat and the rest, will be quite well versed in the value of such, we must remember that these paths are no longer the only ways by which aspirants come to magick, and there are many to whom such ideas are alien.

The concept of these "signs," or gestures holding magickal power is not a new one. Such signs have been used from at least the time of Moses, as shown in Aaron's gesture of blessing, and have carried over throughout history in cultures and religions transcending all borders. Even the Roman Catholic Church has incorporated such symbols into their own rites. In researching the earliest forms of these hand signs one is taken to our Eastern counterparts, where such gestures are revered as "mudras."

The mark of a wise man is acceptance of his weaknesses and willingness to defer to one better versed than he on a given subject. So it is that I asked a friend and brother for whom I have a great deal of respect, Frater Inominandum, to offer his expertise on the subject of these magickal gestures, or mudras, with which he is far better acquainted than I.

"Hand gestures have always played an important part in communication. As newborns we learn to interpret and communicate with gesture several months before words. In 2008 a study by the National Institute on Deafness and Other Communication Disorders (NIDCD) found that gestures are translated by the same regions of the brain that translate words. In ritual, hand gestures can serve to communicate and command spirits and the forces of magic, just as surely as we do with words.

The word mudra in Sanskrit means seal, and while it is sometimes used to denote a mind state, as is the case with Mahamudra, or a certain yogic practices like the Kamamudra (sex yoga), it is used most often to refer to hand gestures used in Tantric ritual. Their use is widespread throughout the east from India where they are used in Hindu, Buddhist, and Jain sadhanas, all the way to Japan where they permeate not only religious practice but martial arts connected with esoteric Mikkyo Buddhism. Their form and function is determined by two factors: the symbolic and the energetic.

Symbolically speaking, many mudras can be interpreted by what they look like. For instance, the mudras for making the eight outer offerings all mimic the form of the offering itself. The offering for Argham and Padyam look like a pitcher pouring water for drinking and washing respectively, Dhupe looks like you are throwing incense on a block, Aloke looks like a candle and flame, Shabda mimics the playing of cymbals and so on. Some mudras are very complex and get used in practical magic, such as the mudras for hooking, pulling, binding, and causing madness that get used in Phurba rituals. In all these cases it is the physical resemblance to a thing that communicates the meaning. These are often accompanied by a word and a visualization such as filling all space with clouds of offering, or sending out hooked lights, and so on.

Some mudras do not have a symbolic resemblance and work primarily through manipulating energy channels (nadis) in the body. Though most yogas work with only three or four of the main channels at a time, there are actually tens of thousands of these channels throughout the body. Much like electrical connections, when complete circuits are made it enables energy to move.

Many people familiar with Pranayama or Qi-gung will be familiar with the idea of putting ones tongue to the top of the mouth in order to complete a circuit. Some mudras connect channels that terminate in the hands in a similar way. This creates different effects that resonate throughout the subtle body and astral environment. For instance there is a mudra used in Mikkyo that sends prana to the belt channel that surrounds the body and bolsters defense against attack. Other mudras, such as the Samashi Mudra used in shamatha meditation create a sense of grounding and calm abiding by circulating energy evenly throughout the body.

Some mudras contain elements of the symbolic and the energetic. The Mandala Offering Mudra used by Tibetan Buddhists everywhere gathers and separates energy into the five elements, but also appears symbolically to represent the four continents surrounding Mt Meru - the central axis of the world. After some chance to experiment with it, I can say that the gesture presented in this work is definitely one of these mudras that operates on a symbolic and energetic level."

Jason Miller

Finally, a word on how this sign or mudra, as we can now knowingly call it, found its way into my magickal repertoire.

It was revealed to me in 1999, during an evocation of the "Four Luminaries" (with whom we will work later in the grimoire proper), wherein I sought to establish communication with the fourth of these angels, Eleleth. While I had by this point succeeded in evoking spirits to visible appearance sans materia, albeit to a much lesser extent than I now know, the rite in question was one where I sought to draw Eleleth into a polished black "shewstone," as Dee termed such devices[1], placed atop a Table of Practice after Trithemius' own design.

While I had little experience with the angels and entities introduced in the Gnostic corpus at that point, and knew not why Eleleth was the ideal spirit unto whom I should address my petition, his name had been presented to me during my daily work with Aset as the best possible ally for me in my present situation.

The rite by which I contacted Eleleth will be found later in this work, and for the sake of brevity I won't repeat it here.

Upon initial contact with Eleleth, which actually took place the second time I performed the rite, he presented himself in a form in keeping with the depictions of him found in the Gnostic traditions, but not as I'd envisioned. About him were his brethren, Harmozel, Oroiael, and Daveithai.

Again summarizing a longer story, having made my entreaty unto Eleleth in the presence of his brethren, I made one final request before bidding him farewell. The request was one that will be familiar to those who work the magicks of evocation, as it is one made frequently unto the spirits with whom we are so privileged as to communicate. I asked if he would provide for me a secret name or other means by which I might, in the future, more swiftly call upon him and be heard at once. If I might be given a more direct line of communication, if you will, whereby I could simply incant as instructed and be assured that my words fell not on deaf ears.

The response I received was delayed by several minutes, and when it came it was to say that, "With the blessings of he whose name is the number of days in your year," after whom this book is now named, I would "be shown a sign wherein two become one, and united in one contain all that is,

---

1   The reason I chose to evoke by way of adjuring Eleleth to appear in the stone as opposed to more corporeally was simply because in this case it was the result that was of dire urgency to me, to wit: his granting my petition; evocation into mediums such as the stone or scrying mirror tends to be more expedient when one's concern isn't bringing such a spirit into his presence but in succeeding in his goal.

all that was, and all that will be, and in the name of he who holds together all, holds the power of his secret name," by virtue of which my workings within this corpus "would be looked upon favorably by all who are called on therein", and my "calls heard, always heard."

In the years since then it has served me well – far more so than any other piece of magickal technology with which I have ever worked. I have never before shared it publicly; it was introduced only to my brotherhood, and even then only incorporated into our weekly rites as a symbol of the source of our power, without ever disclosing to them its origins or uses in evocation magick.

The gesture of which I speak is a symbolic form known to all men and has been revered, respected, worshipped, feared, and beloved since the earliest periods of recorded history. The symbol was known and used by the Sabians, Chaldeans, Khemitians, Babylonians, Greeks, and every civilization and culture since. It is unique among symbols in that whatever the differences in their belief systems, traditions, magickal paths, religions, and forms of worship, the magicians, priesthood, and mystics of all cultures have ever acknowledged its power and connection with the unseen. Presented here, for the first time, is the means by which we can perfectly, physically manifest this eternal symbol.

As will be immediately evident, pictured here is the "pentagram," represented flawlessly on the body of man. As demonstrated here, it is known as the Sign of The Coronastrum. Raised up above one's head toward the heavens it serves "to draw the glory and power thereof, representing the golden sun at its highest peak, Abrasax personified, and the creative force of the universe, allowing the magus to partake and be empowered thereby." At the level of the third eye, whilst having assumed a god-form, it "Crowns the magus as King of all he surveys." At the level of the heart it serves in evocations to assure that the magus is "Heard, always heard." Inverted, with the single point descendant, it is known as The Coronasidus, and it represents "the darkness of the immense night, the blackness and destructive force of the universe in all its untamed beauty," and should be thus employed only when the working is of such a nature.

PREPARATION AND
SECURING OF SPACE

T he observations and preparations in which the magus takes part prior to undertaking a magickal ceremony, however basic or complex it may be, are of great import. What follows is a brief outline of some preparatory steps which I typically use, the value of which I can attest to. While these exercises have been found useful in advancing one's magickal agenda even prior to the commencement of the rite, it is not the practices themselves that yield this result but the mental state which they engender. In any working of this nature it is critical that the practitioner enter a state of mind wholly separate from that in which he spends his mundane life. It is necessary to step outside of his daily existence and all of the commonplace trappings thereof, and to enter utterly into his work; his every thought must be that of a magician rather than a man.. His every act during the time that precedes a ceremony should be a magickal act, and everything he observes should be seen as an act of magick, however unimportant it might seem during his day-to-day life. The landing of a bee on a flower should be regarded as an instinctive yet magickal operation wherein one creature brings new life to another through the mechanism of ritual – i.e., pollination. The rising of the Sun should be greeted as the return of Helios in his chariot, triumphant over the night, hearkening a new day, and not the bothersome call to awaken and go to work rather than remain comfortable in bed. The sole aim of this preparation period and all that it entails is not to fulfill an antiquated set of strictures and regulations by keeping to the letter of the old grimoires, but rather to thrust the magus into an altogether magickal reality.

Many times when conversing with others who have read my books or blog, in venues of a more social nature, I have been asked why, when writing of magick and areas related thereto, I write in a very formal or even anti-quated manner, at times borrowing from the Victorian English common to magickal writings of the late 1800's and typically employing words far distanced from the way I speak in social situations or ordinary conversation. The reason this is so is not because I wish to be seen by readers as some pompous ass, flaunting a decent understanding of the English language or as having a more articulate way than another, but rather because, as explained above, I am elevating all actions related to my magickal work to a higher level of consciousness. When I do enter into a ceremony, I do so having already established the proper state of mind and awareness, having completely removed all the mundane aspects of my life. In practice of magick we endeavor to undertake the art and work of Kings; should we not also speak as Kings when we discuss it?

Having digressed from the topic at hand, let me restate that the primary concern of taking such preparations is not to precisely follow out the instructions and guidelines set forth by our predecessors in the grimoires of ages past. All of the steps one takes in preparation for a magickal ceremony, the days of purification, abstinence, fasting, the ritualized bath and cleansing, the purification of the temple, meditation and prayers, are all working towards building a spiritual mindset wherein we exist not as men working a tedious nine-to-five job, but as beings born of divinity – soon to reach through the barriers that separate us from the celestial and to reestablish our divine right to effect change in our world: the change we desire.

Before any magickal working it is wise to devote a few moments to meditation and the establishment of ritual breathing in order to silence all distractions and idle thought processes and bring one's focus entirely to the matter at hand. I have taken part in several debates wherein the validity of the practice of meditation in this form of work was called into question by "grimoire fundamentalists," who argue that the practice appears nowhere in the grimoires and must therefore be seen as a manifestation of "new age" thought rather than ancient magick. My own belief is that while mastery of meditation is in no way requisite for success, it is a tool we can use to expedite our achievement vastly.

The best "in a nutshell" definition of meditation I have found is Steve Savedow's:

To put it simply, meditation is the silencing of that inner voice that is almost constantly rambling on in a person's head.1

Take for example that which I hold to be the supreme act of magick: Evocation to visible manifestation. This is an act that requires immense focus and single-minded concentration, for any distraction or deviation from the work will inevitably hinder success. The mind, in all of its glory and power, is for most yet untamed, and runs wild and unchecked. During a work such as an attempted evocation, the natural and unavoidable tendency of the mind – however focused you are on the task at hand – is to continually initiate thought processes such as "I wonder if this will work," "Am I doing this correctly," "Did I pronounce that word properly," "Is that shadow a spirit," "I hear a noise; I wonder if that's a spirit, is it really here" and the like. Such unintentional wanderings of the mind are completely detrimental to the working and can prove dangerous. During such a rite these inner voices must be silent and every bit of your focus, both conscious and unconscious, must be singly on the working itself.

Thus, while meditation is not a requirement for success, I know of no other tool or technique as effective as meditation in developing the mastery over one's mind necessary for success in so bold an undertaking as veritable evocation. Developed skill in meditation is also valuable when beginning to delve into the field of Astral Magick, with which we will deal in the chapter on Transcendent Magick.

Despite the value of proficiency in meditation for the magickal practitioner, I will not belabor the subject here by presenting innumerable methods with which the reader can work. Instead I will provide the simplest and most effective exercise of which I know, and trust that the aspirant desirous of further instruction will easily locate a plethora of books or a teacher more qualified than I.

While the exercise that follows can be found in many books, websites, and essays, my own first exposure to it came many years ago via a brief paper entitled "How To Make Contact With Your Inner Teacher." I am unfortunately unsure of the author as there seem to be several versions online, each attributing authorship to a different person. It is, however, derived from the pranayama exercises prescribed by Crowley in *Liber E vel Excercitiorum.*

---

1   Steve Savedow, The Magician's Workbook; A Modern Grimoire. 1995 Weiser Books.

The practice, as I've adapted it, is simplicity itself, and yet it has borne fruit for me more so than any other practice of its sort. For the purposes of the present volume, it is highly suggested that it (or another similar meditative exercise) be adopted by the aspiring practitioner of these magicks and utilized prior to commencement of any magickal working.

1. Bathe, during which you use the traditional words of purification, "Asperges me, Domine, hysoppo et mundabar, lavabis me et super nivem dealbabor"[2] or a variant thereof, and visualize all impurities and weaknesses being washed away in the bathwater.

2. Clothed in loose, comfortable clothing as suited to the ritual that will follow, be seated in a comfortable position, such as that of the Egyptian gods, or with crossed legs atop a pillow.

3. Raise your right hand to your nose and with your forefinger close the left nostril, then inhale for a period of 7 seconds as deeply as you can without becoming uncomfortable.

4. Remain for 1 second.

5. Releasing the left nostril, now close the right with the thumb, and exhale deeply, again for 7 full seconds, leaving no breath left.

6. Repeat 7 times.

7. Remain in this position, focused on your breath alone, allowing no other thoughts to enter your mind, for a period of 5 minutes or more as suits your will.

Prior to commencement of most any magickal working, the Western Tradition dictates that it is incumbent upon us to secure our ritual space. In the Golden Dawn tradition this would include variations of the Lesser Banishing Ritual of the Pentagram, Banishing Ritual of the Hexagram, Invoking Ritual of the Pentagram, and/or variants of Regardie's Watchtower Ceremony. To Thelemic magicians this practice may include the Star Ruby or any of the aforementioned workings. In Jason Miller's *Strategic Sorcery* the term ascribed to this practice is "Zoning," which I hold as far more appropriate than "banishing." By whatever labels it is given, the practice is seen

---

2   The Latin form of the 51st Psalm, meaning, "Thou wilt sprinkle me, O Lord, with hyssop and I shall be cleansed, Thou wilt wash me, and I shall be washed whiter than snow."

as important in nearly every avenue of the Western Mystery Tradition, and the magickal system I've assembled and presented herein does not deviate.

The practices outlined below represent several that I have resurrected from the obscurity of academia. They find their origins directly in this Coptic magick alongside the more advanced rites that will follow, and are therefore best suited for use herewith. They will be found to be far more effective in combination with this corpus than those rites mentioned above which avail themselves of pantheons historically antagonistic to those herein.

The first of these rites will undoubtedly be recognized by some, as it is more widely available than the rest and is found in PGM 824. This rite is to be applied as an all-purpose opening for any and all of the magickal workings contained herein, similar to the function of the LBRP in the Golden Dawn tradition, and may be used in conjunction with the others presented thereafter, or in the case of less complex and involved workings, independent of them (such as in the case of weekly offerings, etc.). This rite is known as Calling Of the Sevenths to Induce Equilibrium and uses the cosmological association of the Greek vowels to the planetary spheres[3] to open the seven gates thereof and bring these forces into perfect harmony within both yourself and your ritual area.

For best results, the Calling of the Sevenths should be performed as would the Middle Pillar (for those familiar with it in its original form), or perhaps the Lightning Strike of the Thelemic corpus. That is to say, using visualizations appropriate to each part of the rite, descriptions of which will be provided following the ritual itself below.

---

3   There are two schools of thought with regard to which of the vowels relates to which planet. In the Saturn-first orientation, chief proponent of which is none other than H. C. Agrippa, we find the following correspondences:

α – alpha, Saturn; ε – epsilon, Jupiter; η – eta, Mars; ι – iota, Sun; o – omicron, Venus; υ – upsilon, Mercury; and ω – omega, Moon. The Moon-first theory reverses the order placing the Moon with alpha and Saturn with omega. Interestingly enough, the only association which remains the same across both systems is the Sun, which is in both placed with iota.

CALLING OF THE SEVENTHS TO INDUCE EQUILIBRIUM

1. Begin standing, facing east, with a moment of meditation, arms at your sides with palms outward. Establish a ritual breathing pattern[4] and visualize a brilliant white body of energy, what some refer to as an aura, about you.

2. Facing East – Stretch out right and left hands to the left, chant "A" (Greek vowel Alpha, pronounced as the "a" in "father"[5]), visualize the same brilliant white light which encapsulates you gathering and expanding at your hands and the gate of the east opening unto you.

3. Face North – Put forward your right fist, chant "E" (Epsilon, pronounced as the "e" in "let") as above, visualize a ball of energy gathering about your outstretched right fist as the gate of the north opens before you.

4. Face West – Extend both hands forward, chant "H" (Eta, pronounced as the "ey" in "obey") and visualize as above, with a ball of energy forming at your hands, and by your will the gate of the west opening.

5. Face South – Both hands holding the stomach, chant "I" (Iota, pronounced as the "ee" in "meet"), visualizing again as above, with the ball of energy taking shape at your hands, and the gate of the south opening before you.

6. Face East - Touch the ends of the toes, chant "O" (Omicron, pronounced as the "o" in "hot"), visualize as above with the gate of the abyss at your feet being opened unto you.

7. Face East – Right hand on the heart, chant "Y" (Upsilon, pronounced as "ou" in "you"). The visualization here is that the aspect of the divine that exists within you is hereby opened, thus from your heart emerges a brilliant light that represents your will.

---

4   To define ritual breathing very simply – perhaps inadequately so – this refers to breathing in for a count of 4 seconds, holding the breath for 4 seconds, then exhaling for 4 seconds. While 4 seconds is my own standard, others prefer 3, 6, or even 9 seconds. It is suggested that, prior to incorporating this form of ritual breath into your work, you experiment and discern which is best for you.

5   Ancient Greek was pronounced in a few different dialects, depending on the region and time period. The pronunciation given herein is the Attic dialect, which would have likely been spoken by magicians practicing this system.

8. Face East – Looking to the sky with hands on the head, chant "Ω" (Omega, pronounced as "o" in "old"). Having opened the gate that is yourself and brought forth your own divinity, you now gaze upward to the heavens and open the gate thereto.

9. Returning your gaze to the East, make above your head The Coronastrum, as previously shown, and powerfully proclaim the following:

ABLANATHANABLA, Take thy place on my right!
AKRAMMACHAMARI, on my left!
DAMDAMENNEOS, behind me!
SENSENKEBARPHAGES, be thou stationed before me!

Be greeted, diadem[6] which is on his head!
Be greeted, seven names who are hidden in it, and
which are **α ε η ι ο υ ω**[7]

The next rite of this sort of which you may avail yourself is one I had previously presented in my contribution to *The Conjure Codex*, Volume I. To it I have given the title "The Adjuration of Metatron." This working, like the former, is drawn directly from the Coptic magickal corpus, and yet also like the former, I have found it of great use in all of my magickal practices.

---

6   Refers to the Crown of God, From Greek "διάδημα"
7   α - alpha, ε - epsilon, η - eta, ι - iota, ο - omicron, υ - upsilon, and ω - omega

The Adjuration of Metatron

1. Facing East, recite:

By the great name of the Father, and to his Glory!
And that of those who stand in his presence,
Athonas Siak Ksas Sabak Kaab Kaesas Ekoe

I call upon thee, O Angel of the Presence!

(The visualization here is of a brilliant and blinding light descending from above and coming to rest just above you)

2. Recite

By Thy Great Names, Given Thee By God,

By Metatron, Draw for me your sword and banish the profane!
By Dynamis, Bend for me your bow against he that opposes me!
By Chasdiel, Cleanse for me the whole of this place!
By Jael, Cleanse for me the depths!
By Yahoel, Cleanse for me the East!
By Megameidan, Cleanse for me the North!
By Pa' aziel, Cleanse for me the South!!
By Na'ariel, Cleanse for me the West!
By Hadariel, Cleanse for me the heights!

At each stage of the invocation, visualize the appearance of a great angel, composed of naught but pure light and energy, at the appropriate place (e. g., when you adjure Yahoel to cleanse for you the East, a glorious angel descends from the brilliant light above you and takes shape in the East of the temple, facing outward, sword in hand, guarding against all enmities. Once Metatron, in each of his forms, has taken his places in your space, consider that you are under the protection of the Angel of the Presence, and that in all that is done therein you shall have his aid.

THE GREATER CALLING OF THE SEVENTHS

The following rite for the securing of space is one of which I make use only in workings of transcendent magick, such as evocations wherein visible appearance is the desired end, or in rites of initiation. While this rite is perfectly acceptable and efficacious in work of lesser consequence, it is altogether unnecessary and might rightly be compared to using dynamite to destroy an anthill. The deities upon which we call in this rite, principally Helios by his most sacred name Achebukrom, and the Graeco-Egyptian "Aion of Aion" are likewise of a transcendent nature, representing the supreme gods of that pantheon.

1. Begin using the Calling of the Sevenths, as outlined above, yet stop at step 9, before the invocation of the guardians of the four directions.

2. Invoke instead as follows:

    "I call thee, who art greater than all, the creator of all, thou, the selfbegotten who seest all but art not seen. For Thou gavest Helios the glory and all the power, Selene the privilege to wax and wane and have fixed courses, yet Thou took nothing from the earlier-born darkness, but apportioned things so that they should be equal. For when Thou appeared, both order and light arose. All things are subject to Thee, Whose true form none of the Gods can see; Who changest into all things. Thou art invisible, Aion of Aion. Come to me Lord, faultless and unflawed, who pollute no place, for I have been initiated into Thy Name."

3. Visualize sealed gates at each of the four cardinal directions, and with divine authority, command them thus:

    "Open, open, four quarters of the Universe, for the Lord of the inhabited world cometh forth. Archangels, decans, angels rejoice. For Aion of Aion himself, the only and transcendent, invisible, goeth through this place. By the name AIA AINRUKHATH, cast up, O Earth, for the Lord, all things thou containest, for He is the storm sender and controller of the Abyss, master of fire. Open, for AKHEBUKRŌM commandeth thee!"

    Repeat this invocation eight times.

The final preparatory rite I will share herein is one which has manifested in many forms over the centuries, most notable of which is Crowley's *Liber Samekh*, or "The Bornless Invocation." In its original form as found on the Stele of Jeu it served as an exorcism, casting spirits from the body of an individual within whom they had taken up residence. This was accomplished by appeal to The *Headless* One, ἀκέφαλος, who in turn would empower the practitioner, giving him the authority to cast out demons in his name. As presented here it serves to remove unwanted influences from the magus' temple and surroundings. It is also of great utility when employed in cleansing one's home or kingdom of predatory or parasitic entities, and ridding oneself of the effects of magickal attack or curse.

I place this rite in this section only reluctantly, for while it is better classified as one intended to secure space, it is not one I would advise the aspiring practitioner of this system to employ with frequency. The reason the rite has been so lauded by magicians from traditions so widely varying as those of the Golden Dawn and, conversely, even those of the left hand path, is because even in forms far removed from the original, it is a very powerful rite.

For all the effort that magicians have put into attempting to define or source the "barbarous words of evocation" found herein, and for all the study we have devoted to understanding why it stands out as one so powerful as to facilitate contact with the Holy Guardian Angel, the truth is that the deity upon whom it calls is of a nature we cannot yet comprehend. καρδία περιεζωσμένη ὄφιν, the "Heart Encircled With a Serpent" is a very potent force, and his name is one to be spoken only with reverence.

THE RITE OF JEU

1. Place white candles at the East, West, North and Southernmost points of the temple.

2. Open the ceremony using the Calling of the Sevenths, adapted as in the preceding rite, to include the invocation of Aion and Helios, and the blasting open of the gates at the will of the magus.

3. Moving counter clockwise, stop at each of the cardinal points, lighting the candle there while reciting:

ARBATHIAO REIBET ATHELEBERSETH ARABLATHA ALBEU EBENPHICHI CHITASOGIE IBAOTH IAO

Subject to me all daimons, so that every daimon, whether of the heavens or air, of the earth or under it, of the land or in the water, might be obedient to me and every enchantment and scourge which is from God.

4. Returning to the center of the temple, facing North, look above to the heavens and recite the above incantation.

5. Gazing downward to Tartarus, repeat the incantation.

6. Clasp your hands at your chest at the level of your heart and again repeat the incantation from step 3.

7. Invoke as follows:

"I invoke you, Headless One, who created earth and heaven, who created night and day, who created light and darkness! You are Osoronnōphris[8], whom no man has seen at any time! You are Iabas! You are Iapōs[9]! You distinguish the just and the unjust! You made female and male! You revealed seed and fruits! You caused men to love each other and to hate each other!

"I am N., your prophet to whom you have transmitted your mysteries as celebrated by Israel! You revealed the moist and the dry and all nourishment. Hear me!

---

8 Ὀσορόννωφρις
9 Ἰαβας andἸαπως

"I am the messenger of Pharaoh Osoronnophris; this is your true name which has been transmitted to the prophets of Israel. Hear me, ARBATHIAO REIBET ATHELEBERSETH ARABLATHA ALBEU EBENPHICHI CHITASOGIE IBAOTH IAO. Listen to me and turn away this daimon.[10]

"I call upon you, awesome and invisible god with an empty spirit, AROGOGOROBRAO SOCHOU MODORIO PHALARCHAO OOO. Holy Headless One, deliver me, N, from the daimon which confounds me[11]. ROUBRIAO MARIODAM BAABNABAOTH ASS ADONAI APHNIAO ITHOLETH ABRASAX AEOOU; mighty Headless One, deliver me, N, from the evils which threaten me! MABARRAIO IOEL KOTHA ATHOREBALO ABRAOTH, deliver me, N, AOTH ABRAOTH BASUM ISAK SABAOTH IAO!

"He is the lord of the gods; he is the lord of the inhabited world; he is the one whom the winds fear; he is the one who made all things by the command of his voice."

"Lord, King, Master, Helper, save the soul, IEOU PUR IOU PUR IAOT IAEO IOOU ABRASAX SABRIAM OO UU EU OO UU ADONAI, quickly, quickly, good messenger of God ANLALA LAI GAIA APA DIACHANNA CHORUN!"

8. Repeat until the spirit of the Headless One fills you, until his essence courses through you, then in a loud, commanding voice, the voice of a God:

"I am the headless one! With my sight in my feet, the mighty one, one with the immortal fire; I am the truth that hates the fact that unjust deeds are done in the world; I am the one who makes the lightning to flash and the thunder; I am the one whose sweat falls as rain so nourishing all that is; I am the one whose mouth is aflame; I am the one who begets and destroys; I am the Favor of the Aeon! My name is 'The Heart Encircled by a Serpent!' Come forth and follow!"

---

10   Modifying this portion as suits your need, e. g., "Listen to me and turn away all whom oppress me," or "Listen to me, banish from my kingdom those who now pollute it, be they man or spirit."
11   Modifying this portion, again, to suit the present need.

9. In the same imperious tone, whilst still enflamed with the essence of the Headless One, command the departure of all that cause you ills or wish you harm, speaking with His voice and issuing this command *as* the Headless One.

PROTECTIVE MAGICK

In this chapter we will be dealing with protective uses of magick, intended to secure the practitioner from magickal attacks, from life's ills, and from enmity and oppression of others. Protective rites, in the form of invocations, prayers, amulets, and charms, have existed as far back into history as can be measured. In the modern world, in which man has all but lost his connection to divinity, forgoing his magickal roots in favor of modern science, such magickal practices are seen as superstition at best. Despite this, to the practitioner of magick – those whose interests in this material are not simply academic, but practical – such techniques are of inestimable value.

Chief among the methods by which the Coptic Egyptians applied protective magick was the creation and consecration of amulets. While the term amulet is often used interchangeably with the word talisman, the two are in fact quite different. A talisman, from the Greek *telesma*,[1] is used by the magus to attract a desired effect to the bearer, such as fortune, love, prosperity, strength, and the like. Conversely, an amulet, from the Latin *amuletum*, is borne to repel undesired affects such as illness, attack, or harm.

Because amulets played a preeminent role in protective magicks during the period with which we are here interested, we will offer a few such examples in this work, all of which I have constructed personally or adapted from originals.

Besides these workings I have also included rites which rely upon the spirits for their protective natures as opposed to tangible materia.

---

1   http://www.etymonline.com/index.php?term=talisman

THE PRELIMINARY RITE OF PROTECTION

The first such rite is derived from London Oriental MS 5525, which I have used in various forms many times. The manner in which I present it here is a form which I utilized to protect a friend who had fallen victim to a rather uninspired curse, laid for him by his former comrades.

1. Begin the rite using the Adjuration of Metatron, as taught in the chapter on Securing of Space, suffumigating with Dragon's Blood incense.

2. When the Adjuration of Metatron is completed, maintain the visualizations created therein, to wit: the presence of Metatron at each side of the temple.

3. Incant thus:

    I adjure you by your name and your power, by your figure and your amulet of salvation and the places where you dwell! By your light wand in your right hand and the light shield in your left, and by the great powers which stand before you! I adjure you, do not hold back and do not ignore, but descend unto me with your amulet of salvation!

    Watch and protect the body and the soul, the spirit and the house of N. son of N, and my loved ones as well! Bring to us life yearly, without any disease! Cast forth from us every evil force and never allow them to approach us! Cast forth from them every evil and every devil, and every Apalaf and Aberselia, and every power of darkness and evil eye, and every eye shutter and chill!

    Cast them away from me, N. and from my family, from my dwelling and children!

    OHI SHAOHI SHASHAOHI SHAIHI SHA AAAO

    OOOOOOO

4. Upon vibration of the *voces magicae* above, let the visualization be of a sphere of brilliant white energy forming above the magus and descending, encapsulating him so that he is fully within.

5. Incant further:

Protect and shelter him, by IAO, by Sabaoth! By the Archangels Michael and Gabriel! By IAO and Sabaoth, Adonai and Elohim, Elemas, Miksanther and Abrasax, by Michael and Gabriel, Raphael and Suriel, by Raguel and Asuel and Saraphuel, I adjure you by your holy powers, watch and protect N.

Thalalmelal, Kokalthaal, Maalbuk, Ananias Setra, Asarias, Misak, Misael Abdenako, Chesenaethi, Chersospaethi, Hilelmilel, Michor!

IIIIIIIAAAAAAA OOOOOOO
IIIIIIAAAAAA OOOOOO
IIIIIAAAAOOOOO
IIIIAAAAOOOO
IIIAAAOOO
II AA OO
I A O

Another manner in which this rite can be used is in empowerment or consecration of an amulet, created as a protective shield. This modification is simplicity itself and is accomplished by adapting the first portion of the incantation, in which we presently find "*but descend unto me with your amulet of salvation!*" to read "*but descend unto me and empower this, your amulet of salvation,*" and altering the visualization used so that the sphere of energy descends not unto the magus but to the amulet, which thereafter becomes aglow and radiates an energy all its own.

The below is an amulet I created for use with this rite. I drew this out on papyrus using a quill pen.

διαφύλαξον τὸν φοροῦντά σου τὴν ἁγίαν σφραγίδα

The ouroboros figures prominently in magickal traditions throughout history; it is one of a few figures that transcends cultures and borders, being regarded as a sacred symbol for as far back as what we now call Hermetic Magick stretches and even further. In the Coptic and Graeco-Egyptian papyri it is used extensively in amulets and talismans. The Greek text in the center above reads, "Protect the wearer of this, your holy seal."

THE RITE OF SOLAR PROTECTION

The following rite is a Solar working invoking the power of the Sun to afford protection from all of life's ills to the magus. It is in the form of a simple adoration to Sol, and employs Judeo-Christian as well as Egyptian deities to achieve its goals.

1. To be performed on Sunday with the rising of the Sun. The temple is to be suffumigated by frankincense and cinnamon, and 5 yellow candles placed throughout – one at each of the cardinal points, and one in the center behind which the magus will operate. Also in the center of the temple place a dish of honey in offering to the Sun.

2. Open the rite by Calling of the Sevenths, the first rite espoused in the section on Securing Space.

3. Circumambulate clockwise from the easternmost point, reciting the associated verse from The Egyptian Book of the Dead as you light the candle there.

    - East - *Homage to thee, O Ra, at thy tremendous rising! Thou risest! Thou shinest! the heavens are rolled aside! Thou art the King of Gods, thou art the All-comprising, From thee we come, in thee are deified.*

    - South - *O Thou Perfect! Thou Eternal! Thou Only One! Great Hawk that fliest with the flying Sun! Between the Turquoise Sycamores that risest, young for ever, Thine image flashing on the bright celestial river.*

    - West - *Thou passest through the portals that close behind the night, Gladdening the souls of them that lay in sorrow. The True of Word, the Quiet Heart, arise to drink thy light; Thou art To-day and Yesterday; Thou art To-morrow!*

    - North - *Homage to thee, O Ra, who wakest life from slumber! Thou risest! Thou shinest! Thou radiant face appears! Millions of years have passed, – we cannot count their number, – Millions of years shall come. Thou art above the years!*

4. After completing the circumambulation and returning to the East, visualize the Sun above you, its glorious rays descending toward you in embrace.

5. Return to the center of the temple, facing East. Ignite the candle there and invoke as follows:

Greetings, lord, greetings, sun of righteousness,
who riseth over all the earth and over the land of Egypt.
You must come down upon this honey, you must take of it!
Prevail upon the twelve powers and their sweetness.
In the name of your great archangel Abraxas,
whose hand is stretched out over his rays,
you must enlighten my heart.
Lord, greetings, Seth Thioth, Barbarioth.
I give thanks to you, our god,
Deiodendea, Yaoth.
Greetings, Lord, the father,
Greetings, Lord, the son,
Greetings, holy spirit,
Yours is the joy, your light has brought it upon me
Light of gladness, Light of the aeons, Light of joy, Light of my eyes,
Lamp of my body,
Lord, God, IAO
Lord, God, Sabaoth.
You must dip your pen in your black ink,
and write upon my tongue your words.
You must give me the sun as a garment,
The moon with which I cover myself as a cloak.
You must give me the boat of the sun,
That it may diminish for me all evil.
You must give me the 7 stars,
you must give me the stuff of the stars,
and I shall be worthy of beholding your face!
You must give me your glory of the sun,
You of the great number,
that it may keep me from all evil.
Yea, for I adjure you,

by the power of Chabarach Rinischir Phunero Phontel
Asoumar Asoumar,
who enlighten the underworld in the evening and the earth in the
morning.
I give thanks to you, O God,
Dediodendeiaoth Lamoir, Serou Seraled, Rima, Aria Nouda,
Damou Menou
Sethioth, Barbarioth

The rite which follows is another of which I have availed myself in creation of an amulet, bearing the resemblance of and calling upon the god Abrasax (Αβρασαξ). While Abrasax is of a cosmology far predating Christianity, he was well known and respected by the Coptic Magicians from whom we take our cues, and appeared frequently on their protective amulets and talismans. He is a constant presence in their magickal formulae, as evidenced by his appearance in the Greek Magical Papyri and the Gnostic "Holy Book of the Great Invisible Spirit."

The amulet I created and consecrated by way of this rite is based on the traditional depiction of Abrasax brandishing "the scourge of power and shield of wisdom," with legs like unto serpents. Underneath this I have the god's name in Greek. These amulets were typically found engraved on stone, which is the manner in which I have created my own, however from experience I can also confirm that engraving on tin and drawing on papyrus are equally effective and more practicable for those who have never before endeavored to engrave on stones.

CONSECRATION OF THE ABRASAX STONE

1. The temple should be established with a single white candle at each of the points of the pentagram; that is to say one before the magus who stands facing east, one each at his left and right, one to the rear left of the temple and one to the rear right. The incense should be frankincense and storax. On the altar, prepare a chalice or wine glass of water into which you have mixed salt and baking soda.

2. Open the rite by the Calling of the Sevenths.

3. Circumambulate counterclockwise, lighting the candle at each point while reciting:

    Anax Sabrex Apemenon Borau Peritrara Nouannoonospetal Kenon Onesinne

4. Return to the center of the temple, facing East. Ignite the incense and invoke:

    Ho! Sax, Amun, Sax, Abrasax; for thou art the moon, the chief of the stars, he that did form them, listen to the things that I have said, follow the proceedings of my mouth, reveal thyself to me, Than, Thana, Thanatha, otherwise Thei, this is thy correct name

    I invoke you,
    The one who governs from heaven to earth,
    From earth to heaven,
    The great one, whose name is the number of days in the year,
    Thou who art our father,
    You, who dwelleth in the light of Eleleth
    You, who preside over the Sun, its rising!

    IIIIIIIIIIIIIIIIIIIIII
    EEEEEEEEEEEEEEEEEEEEEE
    OOOOOOOOOOOOOOOOOOOOOO
    UUUUUUUUUUUUUUUUUUUUUU
    EEEEEEEEEEEEEEEEEEEEEE
    AAAAAAAAAAAAAAAAAAAAAA

OOOOOOOOOOOOOOOOOOOOOOO[2]

Holy, holy, god almighty, creator, invisible one in whose hands are the Scourge of Power and the Shield of Wisdom!

I adjure you by your powers and by your name, by the places where you dwell and the paths you cross! Descend, Great God, and empower thy likeness! Touch my amulet that in your timeless image and by your will may it take life!

5. Dip the amulet into the chalice, incant:

ABRASAX (vibrated 365 times)[3]
By your name I make this amulet so that it may fortify me! I bind the rocks of the earth and tie down the mysteries of heaven! I overcome all demons and harmful spirits in the world, all powers aligned against me and all enmity!
In the name of Gabriel, the mighty angel,
In the name of Yeho'el.
In the name of Yah, Yah, Yah, Sabaoth.
Amen, Amen, Selah

---

2   The seven Greek vowels, vibrated 21 times each. Pronunciations for these vowels are given in the chapter on Securing Space.
3   For exercises of this sort, requiring multiple repetitions of the words of power, my SOP is to use a string of beads containing an appropriate number of beads which can then be counted while chanting the given name. In this case, I use a string containing 120 beads. As I chant the name I count the full string thrice, then repeat the name 5 times more.

A number of traditional Abrasax gem amulets, known as Abrasax Stones

Establishing the Guardianship of Sabaoth

The next protective rite which we will cover is one wherein we find reference to Sabaoth, who is invoked alongside the traditional Judeo-Christian archangels, as well as lesser known counterparts, and charged with the protection of an individual. In the original, the practitioner's intent was to safeguard a third party – a woman – named Alexandra.

The following adaptation adheres closely to the original formula, differing only in that it is here intended to protect the magus himself rather than another.

1. The temple should be prepared as was done with the previous rite. That is to say, with white candles positioned at each of the points of the pentagram and incensed as before. However, in this case, a circle is to be defined on the floor, drawn with natron, and the candles stationed within.

2. The rite is to be opened using the Adjuration of Metatron, following which the magus steps backward to the center of the circle, facing East.

3. Invoke as follows, vibrating each of the capitalized angelic names three times when they appear in the text

   I invoke you SABAOTH, who art above the heavens, who came above ELAOTH, who are above CHTHOTHAI. Protect your supplicant, N, to whom N gave birth, from every daimon and from every power of daimones and from daimonia and from spells and curse tablets.

   I call in the name of the one who created all things;
   I call upon the one who sits over the first heaven MARMARIOTH;
   I call upon the one who sits over second heaven OURIEL;
   I call upon the one who sits over the third heaven AEL;
   I call upon the one who sits over the fourth heaven GABRIEL;
   I call upon the one who sits over the fifth heaven CHAEL;
   I call upon the one who sits over the sixth heaven MORIATH;
   I call upon the one who sits over the seventh heaven CACHTH;
   I call upon the one who sits over lightning RIOPHA;
   I call upon the one who sits over thunder ZONCHAR;

I call upon the one who sits over rain TEBRIEL;
I call upon the one who sits over snow TOBRIEL;
I call upon the one who sits over the forests THADAMA;
I call upon the one who sits over earthquakes SIORACHA;
I call upon the one who sits over the sea SOURIEL;
I call upon the one who sits over the serpents EITHABIRA;
I call upon the one who sits seated over the rivers BELLIA;
I call upon the one who sits seated over the roads PHASOUSOUEL;
I call upon the one who sits seated over the cities EISTOCHAMA;
I call upon the one who sits over the level ground NOUCHAEL;
I call upon the one who sits seated over every kind of wandering APRAPHES;
I call upon the one who sits seated upon the mountains, the eternal god,
EINATH ADONAI DECHOCHTHA, who are seated upon the serpents IATHENNOUIAN.

I call upon you, the one who sits seated over the firmament CHRARA; the one who sits seated over seas and between the two CHEROUBIN forever; the god of Abraham and the god of Isaach and the god of Jakob. Protect N, to whom N gave birth, from malefica and sickness and dangers and trials, and from all suffering and harm!

I invoke you, the living god in ZAARABEM NAMADON ZAMADON, who causes lightning and thunder, EBIEMATHALZERO, the staff of god, under which are trampled his enemies! THESTA and EIBRADIBAS BARBLIOIS EIPSATHO ATHARIATH PHELCHAPHIAON, at whom all things male and all terrible binding spells shudder. Flee from me, your priest, all ye profane, so that you may not bring any stain on me or mine! Approach me not! Oppress me not! Antagonize me not! For I am the man of the highest, before whom trembles all of creation. Holy, powerful and mighty names, protect me from every daimon, whether male or female, and from every disturbance whether those of the night or those of the day.

Amorous Magick

hief among the aims of the magicians of old were the procurement of love and sex, attraction of the opposite sex, and protection of one's relationship from infidelity. Use of magical rites for these ends is a tradition that has carried over to the present time and which remains among the foremost of reasons people develop an interest in magick to begin with. The concept of securing sexual dominion over the opposite sex, becoming irresistible to those to whom you are attracted, and subjugating intimate partners to your will is a fantasy quite familiar to adolescents and teenagers, as well as some long beyond that age. The prospect of this power shifting from the realm of fantasy to reality is an appealing proposition to even the most moral among us – as it has been since the dawn of time – and therefore forms of magick dedicated to accomplishing just that have ever abounded.

Within the Coptic magickal manuscripts as well as the PGM from which we draw, there exist many examples of magickal rites dedicated to these purposes. In this section I will present several of which the modern magus may employ and which have been proven out in my own work or in that of those I've mentored.

The first rite of which we will speak is one that would be termed sympathetic magick by some, in that is makes use of a symbolic representation in the form of a clay figure of the person the practitioner seeks to draw to them or obtain as a lover. Unlike those magickal formulae which seek to turn the heart of a lady[1] unto the magus, what follows here is a *philtrokatadesmos*, that is to say a love-binding-spell, designed not to incline the object of his

---

1   While I refer to the magus herein as male and his desired mate as female, I do so only because this is how it is presented in the text from which this rite is drawn. Any of the magick contained here can be applied equally well by a magus of either gender.

affections to him, but to compel her submission, lest she be unable to find happiness until she relents.

My inclusion of this rite, designed as it was to force the will of another, will likely draw the ire of some among the New Age community who will deem it a work of "black magick" or otherwise immoral. I include it because in study of the ancient texts, be they from this corpus or another, we find frequent works of this sort, and my intent in presenting this system is not to bowdlerize it and offer only what it generally palatable to the masses. Rather I seek to resurrect these magickal practices in their entirety, and leave the relative judgment of good or evil to the student who avails his or herself of them.

I do, however, add a cautionary note to the rite that follows: the practitioner should pay close attention to the maxim "be careful what you wish for, lest that you receive it." In my introduction I wrote that nearly all the rites provided herein had been tested and utilized by myself or my students, and the rite that follows is no exception. While it did produce the immediate result desired by my friend and student, the situation was ultimately not at all what he desired;the loving, affectionate, and sexually submissive girlfriend he received swiftly became a violently jealous lover who could not permit him being anywhere but at her side.

Requisite disclaimers having been offered, the rite of which I speak is quite simple, in fact.

A BINDING LOVE SPELL

Prior to commencement of the rite, on the day of Venus, in the hour of Mars, form of clay or draw on paper the object of your desire, on her knees in submission.

In a subsequent Martial hour of the same Friday you created the above described representation, commence the work thus:

1. Place 13 small pins into the subject, reciting at each insertion

    Aye, lord, daimon, attract, inflame, destroy, burn, cause her to swoon from love and inflame her with passion! Goad the tortured soul the heart of (N), whom (mother's name) bore, until she leaps forth and comes to (name of magus), whom (mother) bore, out of passion and love, in this very hour, immediately, immediately; quickly, quickly. Do not allow (subject), to think of another, nor drink, nor food, but let her come melting for passion and love and intercourse, especially yearning for me in this very hour, immediately, immediately; quickly, quickly.

2. Bury the whole, or the paper on which you have drawn the images of Ares and the woman, invoking thus while doing so

    I entrust this binding spell to you, gods of the underworld, Pluton and Kore, Persephone, Ereschigal and Adonis and BARBARITHA and Hermes of the underworld and Thoth PHGKENSEPSEU EREKTATHOU MISONKTAIK and to mighty Anoubis PSERIPHTHA who holds the keys to the Kingdom of Hades, to infernal gods, to men and women who have died untimely deaths, to youths and maidens, from year to year, month to month, day to day, hour to hour, night to night. I conjure all spirits in this place to stand as assistants to this spell! And arouse yourself for me and go to every place and into every quarter and to every house and bind N, to whom N. gave birth, the daughter of N, in order that she may not be had in a promiscuous way, let her not be had by any but me, nor let her do anything for pleasure with another man, just with me alone!

    Do not let her drink or eat, that she not show any affection, nor go out, nor find sleep without me, N., to whom N. gave birth. I

conjure you, spirits of the dead, by the name that causes fear and trembling, the name at whose sound the earth opens, the name at whose terrifying sound the spirits are terrified, the name at whose sound rivers and rocks burst asunder. I conjure you by BARBARATHAMCHELOUMBRA, BARUCH, by ADONAI and by ABRASAX, by IAO, PAKEPTOTH PAKEBRAOTH, SABARBAPHAEI and by MARMARAOUOTH and by MARMARACHTHA MAMAZAGAR.

Do not fail, but arouse yourself for me and go to every place, into every quarter, into every house and draw to me N until she no longer stands aloof from me for all the time of my life, filled with love for me, desiring me!

The next act of amorous magick with which we will deal is one that most will find far less offensive, in that it is not designed to force the submission of another, but rather to inspire mutual love between them and the practitioner.

The working itself is a consecration of sorts, wherein oil is blessed and thereby empowered so that when worn by the magus in her presence, she is made more receptive to his advances and mutual love born in their hearts.

The oil of which the original author made use would have likely been olive oil[2], perhaps scented with pleasant perfumes.

The working is, as many with which we will work, quite simple, and works in a manner not unlike a prayer which is to be sincerely recited over the oil. The oil is then to be dabbed at pulse points such as the wrist, throat, and the like on any occasion where the magus will likely be in the presence of his lady love.

---

2   One individual with whom I shared this rite reports excellent results having substituted "Ven a Mi" oil, procured at a local botanica. While this is obviously not what was used traditionally, one can see clearly how it could yield comparable results (Ven a Mi is a modified formulation of "Come to Me Girl" hoodoo oil made available in U.S. botanicas).

Consecration of The Unifying Oil

Before beginning, let the magus have prepared a small altar adorned with an image of him and his enchantress together, if one is available, or a representation thereof in the form of their names drawn intertwined. Let white candles be set at either side of this and before it, a dish wherein is contained the oil to be consecrated.

1. On the day and in the hour of Venus, having made offerings of pleasing incenses to Venus as Lady of Love, ignite the candles and recite thrice the following:

   Oil! Oil! O Thou Holy Oil!
   Oil that flows from under the throne of IAO Sabaoth!
   Oil with which Isis anointed the bones of Osiris!
   I call you, oil.
   The sun and moon call you!
   The stars of heavens call you!
   The servants of the sun call you!
   Come, O Holy and blessed oil, so that I may bear you upon me
   So you may bring N. daughter of N. to me, N. son of N.
   You must make my love to dwell in her heart and hers in mine!
   Like a brother and sister, or a bear desirous to suckle her young.
   Yea, yea, I charge you thus!
   By the one whose head is in heaven,
   Whose feet are in the abyss,
   The one by whom the heaven and all of the darkness is hung!
   O Oil, make my love in her heart, and hers unto mine!

2. Pour the oil into a vial or bottle, from which you will draw some when you expect to be in her presence, and wrap in a silken cloth with the picture from atop the altar.

3. Extinguish the candles and end the rite.

What follows is yet another spell intended to bring about a romantic turn towards the practitioner in the heart of she whom he desires. What initially interested me in this rite is that it invokes the legend of the fallen angels and Mastema who was, according to lore, set over them. Mastema is here identified with the biblical serpent who tempted Eve, and it is in this capacity that he is beseeched to likewise fill the subject of the magus' lust with "the devil's passion."

The original of this rite suggests that it is to be incanted over a chalice of wine, enchanting it thereby, which is afterwards served to the woman who is the target of the working, whereupon she is by Mastema filled with passion towards the practitioner. While this method would undoubtedly be more effective, inability to serve the wine to your desired mate (for example, due to distance or some other such unavoidable conditions), should not deter the magus from use hereof. Creating a symbolic representation of the person is adequate, particularly if it consist of a photo.

CREATION OF MASTEMA'S WINE

As with most work of an amorous nature, the following should be performed on Friday and in an hour ruled by Venus. Set up a simple altar on which is placed a chalice of wine with white candles on either side, with incense of sandalwood as suffumigation.

1. Standing before the altar, ignite the incense and candles. Begin the rite thus:

   Heixumarax[1], the one of the iron rod, the one of the lord, from the saltwater, the cataract, whom the whole creation of women obeys, I adjure you with your power and the right hand of the father, the son and the authority of the holy spirit, and Gabriel who went to Joseph and caused him to take Mary for wife that you neither delay nor hold back until you bring to me N., the daughter of N. that I may satisfy my desire for her!

   With desire may she love me! With love may she desire me! May my desire and my love dwell inside her, N., like an angel of god in her presence!

2. In your right hand, raise the chalice and continue:

   For this passion is what Mastema proclaimed! This he threw down into the source of the four rivers on Earth, so that the children of humankind should drink of it and be filled with the devil's passion! This did Eve drink, and was driven to temptation!

   So now do I invoke you, I, N. son of N. that you may bless this wine that is in my hand, in order to give it to N., that she may drink from it and a consuming desire arise within her toward me, and upon drinking she obey me.

   I adjure you by these three names:
   OUSKLEM OUSKLEMA, ANARSHESEF, ELOE ELEMAS YATHOTH!

---

1   Alternatively (due to near illegibility in the papyrus from whence this rite was drawn) where the name Heixumarax appears, one may also substitute Abrasax, **ΑΒΡΑΧΑC**

That you come to me, in my presence, and send desire of me into her like an angel of god, so that if she should not obey me, she be expelled from the good father!

3. If using a photo or other device to represent she for whom you long, place it now into the chalice of wine and incant[2]

    I adjure her by the three names

    IAMALEL, THEMAMAEK, THAE (Repeat eleven times)

4. If serving the wine for consumption by the woman, hold the chalice above your head then incant as above thrice before proceeding.

---

2   I have also seen this modification expanded successfully by placing the photo inside the wine bottle, with the 6 names used in this rite painted thereon, and the whole buried at a location where she may be expected to walk.

The Call of Aphrodite the Queen

What follows is a rite wherein we call upon Aphrodite, Lady of Venus, to assist in matters of love and relationships. The original appears in the PGM as a spell to entreat her aid in matters of divination, however as her governance is of Venus and its specific area of influence, I posited (correctly, as it happens) that the words of power and divine names of which the original made use could more effectively be used to achieve Venusian goals.

1. The temple should be prepared with an image of Aphrodite in a place of prominence atop the altar, surrounded by fragrant roses and incense of rose and sandalwood. Before Aphrodite's image there is to be placed a white candle.

2. The rite is opened by the Calling of the Sevenths.

3. Standing before the altar, light the candle reciting:

    Shimmering-throned immortal Aphrodite,
    Daughter of Zeus, Enchantress, I implore thee, hear me!

4. Light the incense, invoke thus:

    I call upon you, the mother and mistress of nymphs
    ILAOCH OBRIE LOUCH TLOR
    Come in Holy Light and give ear unto my supplication, showing
    Your Lovely Shape!
    I call upon thee ILAOUCH who has begotten Himeros, the lovely
    Horai!
    I also call upon Zeus' begotten Physis of All Things,
    Two formed, indivisible, straight, foam-born Aphrodite.
    Reveal to me Your Lovely Light and Your Lovely Face, O Lady of
    Venus, ILAOUCH.
    I call You, Giver of Fire, by ELGINAL, and by the Great Names:
    OBRI TYCH KERDYNOUCHILE PSIN
    NIOU NAUNIN IOUTHOU THRINX TATIOUTH GERTIATH
    GERGERIS GERGERIE THEITHI.
    I call you, beautiful Aphrodite, by your sacred words
    OISIA EI EI AOE Y IO IAIAIO SO THOU BERBROI
    AKTEROBORE GERIE'IE'OYA;

Bring light and your lovely face and the knowledge of your divine self,
Your countenance, shining with Fire, bearing Fire all around,
stirring the Land from afar
IO IO PHTHAIE THOUTHOUI PHAEPHI

Wealth and Prosperity

Another common use of magick among the Coptic mages, like their counterparts in every civilization and age since, was to secure wealth, prosperity, and fortune for the practitioner. Adjunct to this desire for financial gains were related gains such as respectability, admiration of one's community, and success in business.

In this chapter I present several examples of rites used to accomplish these ends by our ancient predecessors; these have been utilized by either myself or those among my students and contemporaries with whom I've shared them.

The Prayer of the Prosperous

What follows is a simple rite resembling a prayer, overtly Christian in nature, drawn from the Wessely Collection of Papyri. This rite calls upon the archangels through the intervention of their god and Jesus to bring success and fortune. The rite is performed nightly for seven days, beginning on Sunday and taking place each evening in the hour of the Sun.

1. Atop the altar, place a white seven day candle, a censer wherein you will burn frankincense and myrrh or else temple incense, and items having a direct relation to the areas in your life to which you seek to draw success[3].

2. Begin the rite with the Adjuration of Metatron, returning to the place behind the altar facing east.

---

3   Examples include your pay stub, business card, banking account statements, membership documents, and/or cards for organizations to which you belong, etc.

3. Ignite the candle while incanting:

    I beseech you, O god almighty, who is above every temporal ruler and authority and lordship, by every name that is named this night, by the one who is enthroned above the cherubim before you, through our lord Jesus Christ, the beloved child. Hear me, your child!

4. Ignite the incense within the censer, invoking thus:

    I beseech you, O god almighty, send to me, O master, your great archangels, who are appointed for your holy services, Gabriel, Michael, Raphael, Saruel, Raguel, Nuriel, and Anael to stand here before my holy altar and let them accompany me in life!

    During all the hours of day and night, and grant me victories, favor, good luck with N⁴. , success with all people, small and great, whom I may encounter! For I have before me Jesus Christ, who attends me and accompanies me;

    Behind me is Yao Sabaoth, on my right Adonai and left the god of Abraham, Isaac and Jacob; May Gabriel, Michael, Raphael, Saruel, Raguel, Nuriel, and Anael protect me from every demon and enemy, from all wrongs done against me. From every stratagem and plot, for in your name I am sheltered under the wings of the cherubim!

5. Allow the candle to burn down one seventh of its height. Extinguish both it and the incense, if it has not yet gone out on its own, and praise as follows:

    O you king of all the aeons, almighty, inexpressibly a creator, nurturer, master, and lord! And Jesus, almighty, noble child, kindly son, my unutterable and inexpressible name, whose true form remains unseen forever and ever, Amen!

    By the saints remember me, pray for me, bless me! Grant me glory in your name!

6. Repeat each night for 6 more days.

---

4   Here, name your specific requests.

INVOKING THE ANGELS FOR SUCCESS

Adapting it from a longer rite with the same intent, I designed the following ritual to draw business and customers to a venture of mine some years ago which found me importing swords, knives, and other such items from Pakistan and China for sale online. While I had some success prior to the execution of this working, the upswing that followed closely after was such that the effectiveness of my rite could not be disputed.

In the years that have followed I have used this only thrice, as an "ace in the hole", believing – perhaps superstitiously – that overuse thereof would dilute its efficacy. Nonetheless, I have never been disappointed with the boons it has delivered. While it is geared toward one who has their own business, or who is in a position to benefit personally from the success and expansion of the business where he is employed, it may also be modified to draw fortune from sources other than one's place of employment.

1. The temple should be prepared with a circle being defined on the floor, drawn with natron. Inside the circle, white candles should be placed at each of the points of the hexagram, were one laid out within the circle.

    The altar, stationed in the center of the circle facing east, should hold two white candles at the northernmost and southernmost points, between which is a glass of white wine, a sigil you have created to represent your business ventures, and a small denomination of paper money, such as a US $1 bill or its equivalent. Incense of saffron should be burned.

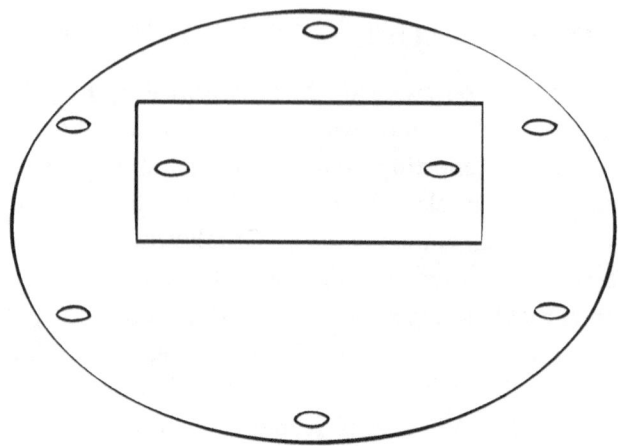

Temple and Altar Layout

2.   The rite is to be performed on Thursday during the 3rd hour of Jupiter. Begin by the Adjuration of Metatron, after which stand before the candle at the easternmost point (before the altar). As you light the candle, say:

> *I beg, I invoke you, lord, our god, almighty, that you send to me from heaven Michael your archangel, that he may gather together the people of this village[5] into the shop of N. child of N. that my fortune be reversed! Glory be to you and your holy words!*

3.   Move counterclockwise to the candle at the upper left corner of the room, repeat as above, but replacing Michael with Gabriel.

4.   Move counterclockwise to the candle at the lower left of the temple and repeat, here invoking instead Raphael.

5.   Move counterclockwise to the candle at the westernmost point, behind the altar, and ignite the candle invoking Suriel.

6.   Moving counterclockwise to the candle at the lower right of the temple, repeat, invoking Zetekiel.

7.   Moving to the candle in the upper right of the temple, repeat the incantation, here invoking Solothiel.

---

5   Modifying this portion as fits your business: such as replacing "gather together the people of this village" with "Send forth to my business customers in droves."

8. Moving back behind the altar, ignite both candles there, invoking Anael.

9. Vibrate thrice ABLANATHALABA.

10. Incant:

    By the Twenty-Four Elders, Holy are their names! Achael, Banuel, Ganuel, Dedael, Eptiel, Zartiel, Ethael, Thathiel, Iochael, Kardiel, Labtiel, Merael, Nerael, Xiphiel, Oupiel, Pirael, Rael, Seroael, Tauriel, Umnuel, Philopael, Christuel, Psilaphael, and Olithael

    Hear my call!

    By the Archangels who stand about my holy altar! Michael, Gabriel, Raphael, Suriel, Zetekiel, Solothiel, and Anael

11. Vibrate thrice AKRAMMACHAMARI.

12. Repeat the statement of intent previously crafted:

    Gather together for me all the people of this village, great small, poor and rich, male and female. Gather them all to N. child of N., to the shop of N., of N. child of N., at once, at once!

13. Raise the glass of wine above your head in your left hand, and the sigil in your right. Incant:

    I invoke' you, Eleath, Elmath, Tet , Atonai, (repeat twice)

    You who have come forth from the mouth of the father who lives forever. You who are the one who is blessed, is glorified, and who lives forever.

    I invoke you, Uriel, Takuel, Akuel, Peskinther, Anaoth (repeat twice)

    The king of those who are blessed, who fear the one who is within the seven curtains, whom the seven firmaments surround, whom the seven angels surround, standing before him, who are these:

    Michael, Gabriel, Raphael, Suriel, Zetekiel, Solothiel, and Anael (repeat twice)

By he who speaks, and the earth moves, he who in the hollow of whose right hand is engraved the great invisible name which is called out, Adonai (repeat Adonai seven times)in whose hand are the souls of people, of men and of women, of reptiles and of beasts and of those that terrify and of those that go upon the ground.

I myself call upon you!

14. Drink the wine, then loudly and commandingly:

    ABLANATHALABA (twice)

    AKRAMMACHAMARI (twice)

    SESEKENPHARPARAKE (twice)

    Gather together for me all the people of this village, great, small, poor and rich, male and female. Gather them all to N. child of N., to the shop of N., of N. child of N., at once, at once!

Following the rite, the wine glass, candle remnants, incense ash, sigil, and money are to be buried outside your residence.

THE RITE OF THE CHARIOT OF HELIOS

What follows is an incantation to Helios, God of the Sun, "Whose is all the Power and the Glory." The rite is to be performed thrice on a single Sunday, each instance thereof being started with the commencement of one of the Sun's first 3 hours.

1. A circle is to be defined on the floor, as always, drawn in natron. The circle, if possible, should be six feet in diameter. At the center of the circle, another circle, one foot in diameter, so that the whole reproduces the Sun's symbol thusly:

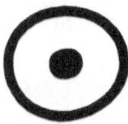

    The altar should be placed immediately to the east of the center circle, so that during the operation proper, the magus may stand within.

2. Atop the altar, define a one foot circle with yet another in the center. An image of Helios[6], hand drawn or copied, should be placed within the center of the circle, with his sacred name ACHEBUKROM written thrice below it. Place three small yellow candles[7], arranged as if on a clock, with one stationed at each of the Sun's hours for that day.[8] In the center place a larger candle, also of yellow or gold, atop the image of Helios so that the melting wax will fall upon it.

3. Incense of frankincense or benzoin, or alternatively a traditional Solar blend should be burned in offering at each of the three performances of the rite.

4. Begin with the Calling of the Sevenths.

5. Recite the Orphic Hymn to Helios:

---

6   Example provided following the ritual outline.
7   Chime candles work quite well here, as they burn down relatively fast.
8   For example, if the Sun's first hour on the day of the work begins at 6:24 am, his second at 1:04 pm and third at 7:56 pm, you will picture the circle on the altar top as if it were a clock, and place one candle at each of these three times.

Hear golden Titan, whose eternal eye with broad survey, illumines all the sky.

Self-born, unwearied in diffusing light, and to all eyes the mirrour of delight:

Lord of the seasons, with thy fiery car and leaping coursers, beaming light from far:

With thy right hand the source of morning light, and with thy left the father of the night.

Agile and vig'rous, venerable Sun, fiery and bright around the heav'ns you run.

Foe to the wicked, but the good man's guide, o'er all his steps propitious you preside:

With various sounding, golden lyre, 'tis mine to fill the world with harmony divine.

Father of ages, guide of prosp'rous deeds, the world's commander, borne by lucid steeds,

Immortal Zeus all-searching, bearing light, source of existence, pure and fiery bright

Bearer of fruit, almighty lord of years, agil and warm, whom ev'ry pow'r reveres.

Great eye of Nature and the starry skies, doom'd with immortal flames to set and rise

Dispensing justice, lover of the stream, the world's great despot, and o'er all supreme.

Faithful defender, and the eye of right, of steeds the ruler, and of life the light:

With sounding whip four fiery steeds you guide, when in the car of day you glorious ride.

Propitious on these mystic labours shine, and bless thy suppliants with a life divine.

6. Vibrate 21 times Helios' sacred name ACHEBUKROM.

7. Light the candle corresponding with the hour in which you are presently operating, as well as that which is atop Helios' image. Raise the Coronastrum above your head and visualize the rays of the Sun descending there.

8. Invoke thus:

Borne on the breezes of the wandering winds,
Golden-haired Helios, who wield the flame's
Unresting fire, who turn in lofty paths
Around the great pole, who create all things
Yourself which you again reduce to nothing,
From whom, indeed, all elements have been
Arranged to suit your laws which nourish all
The world with its four yearly turning points.
Hear, blessed one, for I call you who rule
Heaven and Earth, Chaos and Hades, where
Men's spirits dwell who once gazed on the light,
And even now I beg you, blessed one,
Unfailing one, the master of the world,
If you go to the depths of earth and search
The regions of the dead, send this spirit
From whose body I hold this remnant in my hands,
To her, so and so, at midnight hours,
To move by night to order beneath your force,
That all I want within my heart he may
Perform for me; and send him gentle, gracious
And pondering no hostile thoughts toward me,
And be not angry at my potent chants,
For you yourself arranged these things among
Mankind for them to learn about the threads
Of the Fates, and this with your advice.
I call your name, Horus, which is in number
Equivalent to those of the Fates.

ACHAIPHO THOTHO PHIACHA AIE EIA IAE EIA THOTHO
PHIACA (repeat 21 times)

Be kind to me, forefather, scion of
The world, self-gendered, fire-bringer, aglow
Like gold, shining on mortals, master of
The world, spirit of restless fire, unfailing,
With gold disk, sending earth pure light in beams.

9. Having correctly timed this working[9], the candle at the hour of operation should be nearly extinguished. If it is not yet, remain in meditation until it expires. Extinguish the center candle once it has burnt one third of the way down.

10. Depart the temple, returning and repeating when the next hour of Helios arrives.

Traditional Depiction of Helios

---

9   It is wise to experiment beforehand with the candles you plan to use in order to assure that they will burn down completely within the time allotted, and so that you may pace yourself and your rite accordingly.

The Invocatory Hymn to Hermes

Among the many skills traditionally ascribed to deities of a Mercurial nature is the power to open doors, to guide business and communication, and to further the flow and fluency of all things monetary. Each of these proficiencies make Mercury uniquely qualified to assist the magus whose desire is establishment of long term and steady streams of income, as opposed to onetime windfalls. Mercury is also the planet to whom we credit governance of the magickal arts, as evinced by its association with Hermes himself.

1. On the day of Mercury, and also in his hour, place a white candle before an image of Hermes, offering frankincense thereto.

2. Open the rite by way of the Calling of the Sevenths.

3. Ignite the candle while invoking:

   Hermes, draw near and to our prayers incline, Son of Maia, Teacher of Science, Ruler of mortals, Subtle Minded God, Almighty Heart.
   Celestial messenger, skilled in all the powerful arts,
   With your winged sandals, You travel the roads of heaven,
   Oh Friend of mankind and Prophet of Philosophy, Great Supporter of Life,
   You rejoice in the lithe leaping of the gymnast and in weaving words of trickery,
   Master of all languages, protector of thieves and merchants,
   Whose hand holds the scepter of blameless peace,
   Blessed, profitable God of clever speech, whose aid in words we find,
   Who kindly grants all necessities,
   Dire weapon of the tongue, whom all revere,
   Be present, Hermes, assist our works, grant us eloquence and flawless memories, and conclude our lives with peace.

4. Before the image of Hermes, invoke:

   Hermes, lord of the world, who are in the heart,
   O Circle of Selene, spherical and yet square,
   the founder of the words of speech,
   Wearing golden sandals, turning airy course

Beneath earth's depth, who hold the spirit's reins,
The suns and who with lamps of gods immortal
Give joy to those beneath earth's depths, to mortals
Who've finished life. The Moirai's fatal thread
And Dream divine you're said to be, who send
Forth Oracles by day and night, you cure
Pains of all mortals with your healing cares.
Hither, O blessed one, O mighty son
Of the goddess who bestows full mental powers,
By your own form and gracious mind. And to
Me, N., a pious man, grant your blessings
Open the ways, open the doors, that through them I may pass.

5. Here make an earnest entreaty unto the god, outlining that with which you need his assistance, how it may be accomplished, and the ultimate goal.

6. Vibrate thrice each of the *voces magicae*:

OIOSENMIGADON ORTHO BAUBO NIOERE

KODERETH DOSERE SYRE SUROE

SANKISTE DODEKAISTE AKROUROBORE

KODERE RINOTON KOUMETANA

ROUBITHA NOUMILA PERPHEROU AROUORER AROUER

Mercury

THE TABLET OF MERCURY

Here follows another rite designed to increase one's success in business, trade, and investments by calling upon Hermes. Rather than invoking the god, we instead create a waxen figure, not unlike those used in cursing and binding, except that as used here it represents Hermes himself; it is made with a hollow torso wherein we will store the items used in the spell.

Those readers whose paths have led them to the arts of hoodoo and conjure will find familiar ground in the methods by which this working is carried out. Though these are simple techniques, an individual for whom I created one of these figures was the recipient of a far greater financial boon than anyone else I know, having landed a wholly unforeseen government contract shortly thereafter.

For the rite in question, you will need to obtain a few items:

- Finely ground common ivy plant (*Hedera helix*)

- Roots of the orchid plant, ground as with mortar and pestle to a thick juice consistency.

- Bee's wax

1. The bee's wax must melted and shaped into the form of a man, large enough that a small piece of papyrus along with the aforementioned herbs can be placed inside the torso and sealed. In one hand of the figure should be a staff, the other a pouch, both also formed of wax.[1]

2. Write on a piece of papyrus the following:

CHAIOCHEN OUTIBILMEMNOUOTH ATRAUICH.
Give means and trade to this place, because PSENTEBETH dwells in it.

3. Repeat the following *voces magicae* sacred to Hermes thrice while sealing the papyrus and herbs within the figure using melted wax:

OIOSENMIGADON ORTHO BAUBO NIOERE
KODERETH DOSERE SYRE SUROE

---

1   One need not concern himself overmuch with preparing a sculpture worthy of display. My own skills in this area are rudimentary, and the figure I crafted was no work of art. Put in an honest effort and produce as best a representation of a man as possible, and that will more than suffice.

SANKISTE DODEKAISTE AKROUROBORE
KODERE RINOTON KOUMETANA
ROUBITHA NOUMILA PERPHEROU AROUORER AROUER

4. Once sealed, place the figure atop an altar and make an offering to Hermes in the form of frankincense and wine, giving thanks to him by way of the Orphic Hymn to Hermes, or alternatively the praise utilized in the previous rite.[2]

5. Wrap the figure in silk and store it in a place easily accessible to you, yet hidden to all others and where no one could chance upon it. It is also wise to repeat the offering and thanks as in the previous steps on a monthly basis, and to keep the figure in a well preserved state, not allowing it to be damaged or otherwise defiled.

---

2   The original calls for the sacrifice of a black cock. This, however, I've found to be unnecessary and undesirable.

THE RITE OF THE KINDLING OF THE FOUR LIGHTS

As will be the case with other rites in this book, that which follows calls upon entities introduced in the "Gnostic" traditions. I have often said that I have found more success with the "angels" of this tradition than the more widely known Judeo-Christian archangels, and this working is one of the reasons that this is so. Herein we call on the Four Luminaries, "angels" of the highest God who stand in his presence. The Four Luminaries will be dealt with in a far more powerful way in the final section of this work, wherein we will treat of Transcendent Magick: evocation and invocation.

This rite is to be performed on Sunday evening after the setting of the Sun, in the hour of Helios.

Unlike most other workings in this book, it is advised that for this rite the practitioner not utilize any of the opening rituals to be found in the chapter on Securing of Space, instead employing the following:

- In a censer, place equal parts of frankincense and myrrh incenses.

- In the center of the temple place an altar, bare but for a single white candle which is the sole source of light in the darkened room.

- Light the incense, taking the censer in your right hand, and move to the easternmost point of the temple. Grasp the censer in both hands at chest level and circumambulate counterclockwise nine times, visualizing as you go the smoke of the incense forming a perfectly circular ring around the temple.

- After the circle of protection has taken shape, gaze above as if looking clear through the ceiling, past the treeline, through the stars and clouds, through the highest heavens to the throne of the holy of holies. Breathe in deeply, knowing that the air you inhale is the breath of his lungs.

- Lower your head so that you face the east, and expel your breath. See it as a white flame which mixes with the smoke from the incense, creating about you a ring of fire.

Begin the ritual proper:

1. Standing facing east with your arms at your sides, palms facing outward, meditate briefly.

2. Raise your left and right arms, bringing your hands together above your head in the form of the Coronastrum. Gaze upwards. Visualize the Holy of Holies, "The Man of Light", enthroned above, and a bright white light descending and taking shape at your hands above, then encapsulating you from the peak of the pentagram over your head down to your feet.

3. Invoke:

    Grace dwells in the eternal realm of The Luminary, HARMOZEL, First of The Angels, in whose power are Grace, Truth, and Form! Afterthought dwells in the eternal realm of The Luminary, OROIAEL, Second of the Angels, in whose power are Afterthought, Perception, and Memory!
    Understanding dwells in the eternal realm of The Luminary, DAVEITHAI, Third of The Angels, in whose power are Understanding, Love, and Idea!
    Perfection dwells in the eternal realm of The Luminary, ELELETH, Fourth of The Angels, in whose power are Perfection, Peace, and Sophia!

    I shall praise and glorify you, and he, the Self-Conceived!

4. Lower your hands once again to your sides. Ignite within the censer incense of Abramelin.

5. Invoke:

    I invoke you, O God, Lord of the whole world and of the Earth!
    Who are above the Heavens, beyond that which can be seen!
    God who first gave to man a soul,
    Whose Angels guard the bodies of men!
    You, whose seal is upon those who are burdened by fate,
    Who are great, and exalted over the midpoint of the seas!
    Who establishes all, who guides all, who are the father of even the gods.

    By your Four Glorious Luminaries, Harmozel, Oroiael, Daveithai, and Eleleth
    By Abrathona, Ya Ya, Greatest of Gods
    Who rides upon the powers, who casts out the demons!

6. Lower yourself to kneeling, right knee to the abyss, left to the heavens, form at chest level the Holy Sign and invoke

I adjure you, O Father, by your names and your words,
As you set Harmozel over the First Eternal Realm, Set me over my own
As you set Oroiael over the Second Eternal Realm, Set me over my own
As you set Daveithai over the Third Eternal Realm, Set me over my own
As you set Eleleth over the Fourth Eternal Realm, Set me over my own

As these are the four who stand before the Self-Conceived God,
Place before me my peers! Place before me all men!

CURSES

The next group of magickal rites with which we will deal are those of offensive, cursing, or destructive magick. Despite this type of magick having been maligned and seen throughout history as immoral, evil, heretical, or blasphemous – so much so that even practitioners of the magickal arts shy away from their use and condemn those who dare to make use thereof – we find no shortage of these works in any magickal corpus. From the admonition of King Tutankhamen that *"Death will slay with his wings whoever disturbs the peace of the pharaoh,"* to the defixiones tablets of our Greek ancestors, cursing another has ever been a staple of magickal praxis. Indeed harmful or "baneful" magick may even represent one of the largest fields of magickal praxis we find in the ancient texts, with some 1600 examples thereof surviving, dating from as far back as 500 BCE.

Of frequent use in rites wherein the destruction of another is the goal, as well as in magick for love, attraction, and for other means, is the clay figure. While modern practitioners tend to associate these miniature representations of people with hoodoo, the fact is that clay figurines have been used in magick as far back as recorded history permits us to delve. The last of the native Egyptian pharaohs, Nectanebo, was known as a great magician who defeated invading armies by visiting a sacred room within his palace, crafting clay figures of his enemies and the ships upon which they sailed and assailing them with magickal incantations, after which the winds would inevitably sink his enemies' convoy. The 13th century historian Abu-Shaker tells us that much of the success of Alexander the Great was secured through use of waxen figures of his enemies given him by Aristotle, to which Alexander would do magickal harm.

While I do not condone the use of predatory magick for its own sake, or to right imagined wrongs, unjustly empower tyrants, or arbitrarily strike down perceived enemies, I am far from one of those New Age "touchy feely" sorts who believe that any use thereof is evil or constitutes "black" magick. I view works of this type as simply another tool with which the magus can build, and more importantly protect, his Kingdom. It can be wielded as a weapon or serve as a deterrent to those who would do him harm.

The Coptic papyri from which the thrust of this volume is drawn, like nearly any other corpus of which we are aware, contain numerous examples of magickal works designed to curse, avenge, bind, or otherwise destroy another. Herein I will present several, along with instructions for implementation thereof in the modern day. As mentioned earlier in this volume, you will find nothing herein that has not been used – and successfully so – by myself or someone of my close acquaintance, and the works in this chapter are no exception.

I do caution any who would make use hereof that while I find the imagined law of karma laughable and inexistent, it is wise to exercise discretion when working in harmful forms of magick. This I say not for fear of some universal blowback by which the harm one has done is brought back upon them, but because however proficient you may become in this form of magick, there is always one more so. While karmic repercussions will certainly not strike you down, one more skilled or experienced than yourself very well may.

THE SUMMONING OF SET-TYPHON TO STRIKE ONE'S ENEMIES

The first rite we will cover is one with which the reader may be familiar, as I have discussed it to a lesser degree elsewhere. The rite in question forms Col. XXIII of the Leiden Papyrus, and calls upon Set-Typhon to bring destruction and ruin unto one's enemies. The variant thereof which was previously published in *Crossroads*, directed at three specific individuals and designed to reverse malefica they had authored towards another, is here modified to serve as less a reversal and more of an attack.

1. Prepare the temple by placing a black candle atop the altar, underneath which you have set an image of the subject of your work, or another representation of him/her.

2. The candle may optionally be dressed in an appropriate oil, such as black arts or crossing oil. Likewise the photo of the intended target may also be bound in devil's shoestring.

3. Burn dragon's blood incense in offering to Set-Typhon, he upon whom you will be calling in this rite.

4. Invoke Set-Typhon as follows

    I invoke thee, who art in the void air, terrible, invisible, and almighty! God of Gods, dealing destruction and maker of desolation! He that hatest the household well established, from which thou were cast, Egypt, to which you were entitled! "He that destroyeth all and is yet unconquered" is thy name! I invoke thee, Set-Typhon, by thy words of power which thou canst not refuse to hear!
    YOERBETH, YOPAKERBETH, YOBOLKHOSETH, YOPATATHNAX, YOSORO, YONEBOUTOSOUALETH, AKITIOPHI, ERESKHIGAL, NEBOPOSOALETH, ABERAMENTHOOU, LERTHEXANAX, ETHRELUOTH, NEMAREBAM AEMINA!

5. Upon the arrival or detection of the presence of the god, praise thus

    You are the great god who carries away the soul,
    Who eats hearts and who feeds upon offal,

the guardian who is in the darkness,
the guardian of the Seker boat.
Who art thou then? You are Seth; You are the soul of Geb.

6. Deliver the charge as follows, modifying as suits the circumstance

Come to me and approach! Hear my words! Strike down N with
frost and fire, and bind him that he shall wrong me no more!
Strike him down in thy might and strength, bring to him ruin
and shame! Tear from him his limbs! Deliver unto me the head of
my enemy and to Great Set-Typhon shall I sacrifice! Thy praises
shall I sing!

Among the rites of cursing found in the Coptic Papyri are many which resemble prayers, such as that which we will provide next. These adjurations to ancient deities were typically written on papyri or other surfaces and buried, after which they were considered delivered to the deities unto whom they were addressed. In this case, reference is made to "Lord Sabaoth," as well as Judeo-Christian archangels. Also of note is that the legend of Cain's slaying of his brother Abel is mentioned herein, as is the suffering of Job and the betrayal of Judas, furthering the biblical associations.

Frequently additional curses were appended, such as in the case of the rite which follows, which direct the forces called upon against any who may happen upon the buried spell and dare to open it: "*Whoever shall open this papyrus and read what is written inside, may all those things written in it descend upon him.*" This addendum has been omitted from the ritual as outlined below, simply because it was omitted when I originally used it some years ago.

This working is one of which I am particularly fond, primarily because of its utter simplicity. The incantation is written on a sheet of new papyrus[1] while repeating the words thereof, an offering is made to the spirits in whose hands we seek to place the burden of its achievement, and thereafter it is "delivered" by way of burial.

Another aspect of this rite that I find endearing is that it is as versatile as it is simple, and can be expanded infinitely. Placing the papyrus in a bag similar to those used in hoodoo-style mojo hands accompanied by coffin

---

1   Readily available and inexpensive, directly from Egypt, online. Another convenience afforded the modern magician by way of the internet.

nails, a photo of the target bound in barbed wire, and other such items can indeed add another dimension, as well as making it more familiar to practitioners of hoodoo, rootwork, and conjure.

The rite, as used by myself, follows. The image, of course, does not depict that which I used therein, as that remains buried. It is instead one written to illustrate the method.

Creation of a Modern Defixio

1. Prepare the incantation which follows by writing it upon a new sheet of papyrus using ink into which you have mixed crushed habanero powder. The incantation provided below should be repeated while it is written, this being done on Tuesday in an hour ruled by Mars, in a room lit only by black candles.

God of heaven and earth! Yea, god of heaven and earth! Lord, you are the one who knows those things which are secret and those which are revealed.

God, you are the one who I call to perform my judgment against all those who oppose me. My father Michael, my father Gabriel, Suriel, Gunuel, Raphael!

Not by my power, but by the power of the lord Sabaoth and all those whose names are recited, you shall appeal to the god of heaven and earth.

Trample my enemy, N, Bring him down for he is acting like a demon. God, may you bring down N.

Render him friendless, in prison, like a bronze chain, as I produce these trusty words.

Any person, everyone, who brings bad things upon me and every one who calls my name in evil, those who curse me, all of them, O great God, you who shall perform my judgment against them all, lord, god – you shall bring all of them down, all of those who oppose thy son!

Lord, do not neglect my spell and my request, for they have mistreated me.

You must bring him down from his heights, just as he sought to do to me!

Lord Sabaoth, do not neglect me. The cherubim, the seraphim, the ten thousand angels and archangels shall appeal to the god of heaven and earth, and he shall perform my judgment against everyone who opposes me. Anyone who curses me, you must bring down and abandon him to demons.

Yea, true, beloved savior!

Yea, consubstantial trinity!

Let me watch N's demise!

let me watch him, being afflicted by the spirits of the world.
You must bring upon him all the sufferings of Job.
Number them with Judas on the day of judgment.
Liken them to those who have said, "His blood is upon us for three
generations."
You must liken them to Cain, who murdered Abel!

2. Having prepared the curse thus, fold it thrice and seal the papyrus with the melted wax of the candles.

3. Bury the papyrus, sealed, either as is or having been placed in a bottle or small pouch, incanting as follows:

"I deposit with you this curse, great chthonic gods and Pluto;
UESEMIGADON; Maiden Persephone, Ereschigal sister of Inanna
and ruler of the underworld, the BARBARITHA; THOOUTH
PHOKENTAZEPSEU AERCHTHATHOU MISONKTAI
KALBANACHAMBRE; powerful Anpu, PSIRINTH, holder of the
keys to Hades; gods and demons of the underworld! I adjure you, one
and all. Rouse yourself for me and seal my curse, so that for as long
as this tablet shall be in your possession, what it contains will come
to pass!

ROMAN RITE OF REVENGE

While the intent is that the bulk of the present volume consists of rituals from Coptic Egypt, the working which follows represents one of a handful I've included from other sources; in this case a collection of nearly 60 such cursing or binding rites discovered in burial tombs along the Via Appia of Rome. This, and the other few rites drawn from non-Greco-Egyptian sources, have been included due to their remarkable compatibility and similarity with those that form the majority of this book.

Of interest to me is the fusion of cultures this charm represents, making use as it does of the name Adonai – with which the reader is undoubtedly familiar – alongside the Egyptian Osiris and Ra as well as the name of a demon found frequently in later texts, Eulamon.

Traditionally this binding was written on papyri, rolled, sealed in a tomb as previously mentioned, or else accompanied by several nails and buried.

1. Prepare first the spell as provided below, writing it on a sheet of new papyrus during the day and hour ruled by Mars.

2. Roll the papyrus as you would a scroll, reciting as you do:

    EULAMÔN, restrain him!
    OSIRIS, APOPHIS, MENE, RA!
    Archangels come! In the name of the underworld one, so that, just as I entrust to you this impious and lawless and accursed N., whom his mother N. bore, so may you bring him to a bed of punishment, to be punished with an evil death, and to die within five days[2]. Quickly! Quickly!

3. The papyrus is then to be buried with 9 nails in a cemetery, or if this is impossible then first placed in graveyard dirt and only thereafter buried elsewhere. While it is committed to the earth, the following invocation is to be repeated, and an offering of incense made to the deity upon whom it calls.

    You, Phrygian goddess, nymph goddess, ADONAI, IAO EKATOIKOUSE, I invoke you by your secret names that I know, so that you may help me and restrain and hold in check N. and

---

2 If the severity of the curse for which this rite was traditionally used disconcerts the potential practitioner hereof, it can be modified to reflect a desired sentence of a lesser degree.

bring him to a bed of punishment, to be punished with an evil death, to come to an evil condition, him whom his mother N. bore. And you, holy EULAMON, and holy Characters, and holy assistants, those on the right and those on the left, and holy Symphonia! These things have been written on this tablet so that, just as I entrust to you this impious and accursed and ill-fated N., whom his mother N. bore, bound, tied up, and restrained within five days, because I invoke you by the power that renews itself under the earth, the one that restrains the planets and OIMENÊBENCHUCH BACHUCH BACHACHUCH BAZACHUCH BACHAZACHUCH BACHAXICHUCH BADÊTOPHÔTH PHTHÔSIRÔ.

The following is a rite traditionally used as a curse tablet, or defixio, serving as a binding of an individual's aggression toward the practitioner. It has been suggested that the rite was originally to be carried out in a cemetery, or at a gravesite, a reasonable assumption given that portions of the incantation are addressed "to you who lie here" and "daimones, buried in a single grave, violently slain, untimely dead, or improperly buried." Also of interest is that in this rite we find variants of the widely known "Osorronophris," which the reader will undoubtedly recognize from The Stele of Jeu, or The Bornless Ritual, *Samekh*, et. al., which in the original is rendered as "OISORNOPHRIS."

While the practice of carrying the rite out at graveside may indeed lend additional potency to the rite, it does not appear a stricture thereof, as when used by a sister with whom I shared it; it was carried out in a wooded area with but a jar of dirt from a local cemetery spread atop the tablet as she buried it. Despite this deviation from the original practice this rite proved quite useful, further evincing our assertion that while adhering as closely as practicable to the original methodology is best, excellent results are quite attainable when such adaptations are necessitated by the change in times.

This working, in its original form, differs greatly from those with which we have thus far dealt in that it serves not to harm the target but rather to cause them to forget their aggression towards the practitioner and abandon their attempts to do him harm. While the incantation which follows can be readily modified to transform the working into a piece of attack magick, it is in the original form that it was used by my associate, and that therefore is what I offer here.

CREATION AND EMPOWERMENT OF THE DEFIXIO, II

1. On the day and in the hour of Mars, in a room lit by black candles and suffumigated by Martial incense, call first upon Mars by way of the Orphic Hymn dedicated unto him.

2. On a tablet of ceramic or clay, inscribe your curse, a product of your own creation written to express your desired end, while repeating it vocally.

3. When the tablet is completed, take it along with the remnants of the candle and ashes of the incense and an amount of graveyard dirt sufficient to cover the surface of the tablet, to the location selected for the interment.

4. Dig a hole 9 inches in depth. Place the tablet, candles, and incense ash therein, with the graveyard dirt covering the surface completely so that no part of it is exposed.

5. Begin slowly filling in the "grave," while speaking the incantation:

    Daimones under the earth and daimones whoever you may be, you who lie here and you who sit here, since you take men's grievous passion from their heart, take over the passion and hatred of N. which he has toward me, N. and his anger; and take away from him his strength and power and make him cold and speechless and breathless, apathetic toward me!

    I invoke you by the great gods, MASOMASIMABLABOIO MAMAXO EUMAZO ENDENEKOPTOURA MELOPHTHEMARAR AKOU RASROEEKAMADOR MACHTHOUDOURAS KITHORASA KEPHOZON, the goddess ACHTHAMODOIRALAR AKOU RAENT AKOU RALAR, ALAR OUECHEARMALAR KARAMEPHTHE SISOCHOR ADONEIA of the earth CHOUCHMATHERPHES THERMOMASMAR ASMACHOUCHIMANOU PHILAESOSI gods of the underworld, take over from N. the passion and anger they hold toward me, and hand him over to the doorkeeper in Hades, MATHUREUPHRAMENOS, and to the one who is appointed over the gate to Hades and the door bolts of heaven, STERXERX ERER, the earthshaker ARDAMACHTHOUR

PRISGEU LAMPADEU, and bury in this mournful grave the one whose name is written on this defixio which brings about silence. I invoke you the king of the unhearing, unseeing and voiceless daimones. Hear the great name, for the great SISOCHOR rules over you, the ruler of the gates to Hades. Of my opponent N. bind and put to sleep the tongue, the passion and the anger he holds toward me lest he oppose me in any matter. I invoke you daimones — buried in a single grave, violently slain, untimely dead, not properly buried — by her who bursts forth from the earth and carries down into the grave the limbs of MELIOUCHOS and MELIOUCHOS himself. I invoke you by ACHALEMORPHCPH who is the only god of the earth OSOUS OSORONOPHRIS SERAPIS, do whatever is written herein. O much lamented tomb and gods of the underworld and Hekate of the underworld and Hermes of the underworld and Plouton and the infernal Erinues and you who lie here below, untimely dead and unnamed, EUMAZON, take away the voice of he who is opposing me,

I deposit with you this charge and spell to make N. silent, and give over his name to the infernal gods. ALLA ALKE KE ALKEO LALATHANATO, three-named Kore. These shall always carry out my desires for me, for I know well their names. Awaken yourself for me, you who hold the infernal kingdom of all the Erinues. I invoke you by the gods in Hades, OUCHITOU, the dispenser of tombs, AOTH IOMOS TIOIE IOEGOOEOIPHRI, who in heaven rule the upper kingdom, MIOTHILAMPS, in heaven, IAO, and in the kingdom under the earth, SABLENIA IAO SABLEPHDAUBEN THANATOPOUTOER. I invoke you, BATHUMIA CHTHAORGOKORBRA ADIANAK KAKIABANE THENNANKRA. I invoke you gods who were exposed by Kronos, ABLANAHTALBA SISIPETRON, take over N. the opponent of me, OEANTICHERECHER BEBALLOSALAKAMETHE, and you, earthshaker, who holds the keys of Hades. Carry out for me this curse!

TRANSCENDENT

Having presented at some length the rites of practical magick I've drawn from the Coptic and Graeco-Egyptian papyri and provided the reader with a full system with which to work, we must come now to those workings which I term transcendental, or higher magicks.

Many authors throughout history have used this term to denote varying aspects of magickal practice. Everyone from the venerable Eliphas Levi and later A. E. Waite to modern day theoretical magicians employed the term "transcendent magick" in definition and classification of magical works they considered to be of a higher level, a more divine or holy class, or one wherein no trace of "black" magick has contaminated the praxis.

In my own system of belief and practice, however, transcendent magick simply refers to those workings wherein veritable communication with spirits, be they holy or diabolical, angelic or demonic, is sought, such as True Evocation. While much of the magick in this grimoire calls on and indeed relies upon their intervention to achieve one's ends, the appearance of the spirit is not required, nor is communication. The success of the rites taught prior to this point should be determined solely by the results derived therefrom. True Evocation, in the system I teach and as outlined here as a form of transcendent magick, is evocation wherein the ultimate goal *is* the appearance of the evoked and the establishment of communication therewith. To put this in the words of another:

> "High magic is an attempt to gain so consummate an understanding and mastery of oneself and the environment as to transcend all human limitations and become superhuman or divine. Low magic is comparatively minor and mechanical, undertaken for immediate worldly advantage, to make money or take revenge on an enemy or

make a conquest in love. It tails off into the peddling of spells and lucky charms."

Richard Cavendish

Another segment of practices which I've termed transcendent are magicks of invocation, wherein the magus becomes a vessel for a deity, thereby sharing his body, consciousness, and being with the invoked and partaking of the divinity and power thereof.

Besides evocation and invocation proper, there is another magickal work which is most worthy of this exalted status, and that is initiation. I refer not to those initiations one receives at the hands of his peers in any of the extant magickal orders[3], but those carried out by the spirits themselves. In this volume you will find a very early example of an initiatory rite, attributed to the Master Yeshua[4], taken directly from the Gnostic scriptures and termed "Triune Baptism"; it contains the magickal seals and signs necessary to affect true spiritual initiation and magickal awakening.

This "Triune Baptism" is one of two rites found in this chapter which have been designed as workings of astral magick – that is, magick performed on the Astral Plane as opposed to the Physical. In the present day, astral magick has been unjustly grouped with the new age idiocy – for which I am so public in my loathing – by those who know not its true value. It therefore behooves me to explain the world of difference between true astral magick and the latter forms which I describe as mental masturbation. The astral magick with which we will work in the present volume is accomplished either through conscious astral "projection," or "mental projection," both of which are effective for our purposes. Astral projection refers to conscious, willful separation of the consciousness from the physical body, enabling the individual to travel in a plane wherein the rules of time and space to which we are accustomed no longer apply. Donald Michael Kraig explains in depth the ritual and Qabalistic processes by which magick on the Astral Plane works in his classic introduction to ritual magic *Modern Magic*, however the

---

3   Although these initiations, when the initiator is sufficiently ascended and developed in his skill and praxis, are also of inestimable value. The problem in the present time is that identification of such a reputable group is difficult, our community being plagued by demagogues who are too deeply mired in accusing their rivals of lacking magickal power or initiatic authority.

4   The true name of Jesus.

entirety of his thesis – which I share – can be summed up in the following quote from Lesson 5 of that work:

> *"For anything to exist on the physical plane it must first exist on the Astral Plane! Therefore, in order to create anything and bring it into your life, all you have to do is create it in the Astral Plane. This is the underlying principle of all Grey Magick."* [5]

Magick on the Astral Plane, and more specifically initiation taking place there, are not concepts unique to this book. Steve Savedow, in his excellent work *The Magician's Workbook: A Modern Grimoire* contends that:

> *"...an initiation can never be self-performed, save for one exception, and this is no simple task. The only acceptable form of self-performed initiation must be performed by the individual on the astral plane....*

> *"....What is required for the uninitiated is that you project yourself above the terran plane, and astrally create a temple with specific layout and detail, with every required object in its appropriate place...."*[6]

Savedow then goes on to modify a traditional rite of initiation in the Golden Dawn Tradition for execution in the Astral Plane.

Those among the rites that follow which make use of the Astral Plane as their temple have been faithfully recreated from the originals, and I am confident that on practice therewith the Magus will find them quite potent.

Because the rites contained in this section are of a higher level than those that precede them, it behooves me to briefly address some preparations which the practitioner of this system can use to prepare himself for the experience. It is assumed that those in whose hands this work finds itself will have some familiarity with at least the fundamentals and thus this section may well be redundant for some, but in the interest of being as thorough as possible it is included nonetheless.

While a 3-day preparatory period isn't strictly necessary, and it may well be shortened to accommodate everyday life and responsibilities, it is that which I personally use and is therefore what I present here. As with all things, the reader is encouraged to experiment and adapt as suits his own will.

---

5   Kraig, Donald Michael. Modern Magick. St. Paul: Llewellyn Publications, 2002, 219.
6   Savedow, Steve. The Magician's Workbook. York Beach, ME: Samuel Weiser, 1995, 201.

DAY 1.

- The magus begins a progressive fast[7] which commences with meals limited to whole foods, fruits & vegetables, etc.

- In addition to the fast, 3 meditation sessions of 30 minutes each should be undertaken.

- If the magus has reached the level of ascent wherein he has made conscious contact with his Holy Guardian Angel, or else the Supernatural Assistant of the PGM, the Genius, any patron deities, or another such protective spirit, offerings of frankincense or storax should be made daily while reciting the following prayer (known as the Prayer of the Messenger Paul):

Grant me your mercy, My redeemer, redeem me, For I am yours. I came from you. Yours is my mind, Give me birth. Yours is my treasure, Open for me. Yours is my fullness, Accept me. Yours is my rest, Give me unlimited perfection. I pray to you, You who exist and who preexisted, In the name exalted above every name, Through Yeshua, the anointed O Lord of Lords, King of the Eternal Realms. Give me your gifts with no regret, Through the human child, The spirit, The advocate of truth! Give me authority, I beg of you! Give healing for my body, as I beg you, Through the word of the gospel. And redeem my enlightened soul forever, and my spirit, And disclose to my mind the firstborn of the fullness of grace. Grant me what the eyes of the angels have not seen, What the ears of the rulers have not heard, And what though hast not yet arisen in the hearts of people, Who became angelic After the image of the animate god When it was formed in the beginning. I have the faith of hope, And bestow upon me, Your beloved, chosen majesty, You who are the firstborn of the first conceived, And the wonderful mystery of your house. For yours is the power, and the glory, and the praise, and the greatness, forever and ever

For those who have aversions to the previous prayer, what follows is one taken from the PGM which may be substituted

---

7   It is, of course, imperative that the health and well-being of the magus be considered when contemplating any sort of fast. Consulting your physician to determine if such action would be unduly dangerous for you is a must.

Greetings, O Lord, thou who art the way to receive favor for the universe and for the world in which we dwell.

Heaven is become a place of dancing for thee: ARSENOPHRE, O King of the Heavens!
Greetings, O Lord, thou who art the way to receive favor for the universe and for the world in which we dwell.
King of the Heavenly Gods, ABLANATHANALBA, thou who possesses righteousness: AKRAMMACHAMARI, Gracious God! SANKANATHARA, Ruler of Nature!
SATRAPERKMEPH, origin of the heavenly realm, ATHTHANNOU ATHTHANNOU ASTRAPHAI IASTRAPHAI PAKERTOTH SABAOTH ERINTASKUOUTH EPHIO MARMARAOTH.
Let my ability to speak not leave me. Let every soul pay attention to me, for I am PERTAO MECH CHACH MNECH SAKMEPH, Gods, ABLANATHANALBA, thou who possesses righteousness!
Grant to me that which be thy will!

DAY 2.

- Progressive fast continues, limiting the day's nourishment to fruits, vegetables and pure water On this day the Magus will clean the temple physically, using Florida Water, "Holy Water" if it suits his will, or in my case, water from the Nile River. The circle in which he will perform the work is also constructed, consisting solely of a single line unless his will leads him to adorn it with other devices. The circle in my case was created from homemade natron, recipes for which can be readily found online. Daily meditation sessions continue with 3 repetitions.

- Repeat offerings as before.

DAY 3.

- Abstinence from all forms of distraction including TV, internet, phone, etc. This day is spent in meditation, reflection, and relaxation to prepare oneself for the following day's work.

- Progressive fast culminates with all intake besides water being ceased 24 hours prior to the rite.

- The temple wherein the ceremony will take place shall be thrice cleansed magickally, using the rites to be found in the first chapter on Securing the Space, selecting for use that which applies best to the working to follow. After each of the three sessions, quit the temple.

"These mysteries which I shall give unto you, guard them and do not give them to any man save he who is worthy of them. Give them not to your father, or mother, or brother or sister, and not to your relation. Give them not for food or for drink, for a woman or for gold, for silver or for anything at all which is of this world….

…Neither give them to those who serve the eight powers of the great archon, who are those that eat the menstrual blood of their impurity by saying "We have the knowledge of the truth and we pray to the true god, however their god is wicked…" [8]

The following rite, along with one that will appear later in this chapter, are drawn from the First and Second Books of Jeu. The Books of Jeu represent two sections of a 47-leaf papyrus corpus called the Bruce Codex, so named because it was discovered by a James Bruce during his travels in Egypt in 1769.

While academia has examined the Bruce Codex exhaustively, it has largely evaded the considerations of those whose interests lie in modern magickal praxis. Having devoted considerable time and effort to the study of this manuscript, and having used portions thereof to success exceeding that which I've experienced in any other magickal work, I can attest that the Books of Jeu (and "The Untitled Texts" which accompany it in the Bruce Codex) contain mysteries and secrets that would take a lifetime to decipher. Further, the magickal practices hidden in James Bruce's 47 leaves are of a power I have yet to experience elsewhere.

Herein I will present only two of the dozen magickal workings I have developed from *Codex Brucianus,* and yet in these two I am confident that indisputable proof of the corpus' validity can be found.

---

8   The Master Yeshua, addressing his disciples prior to their threefold baptism, as recorded in the Second Book of Jeu.

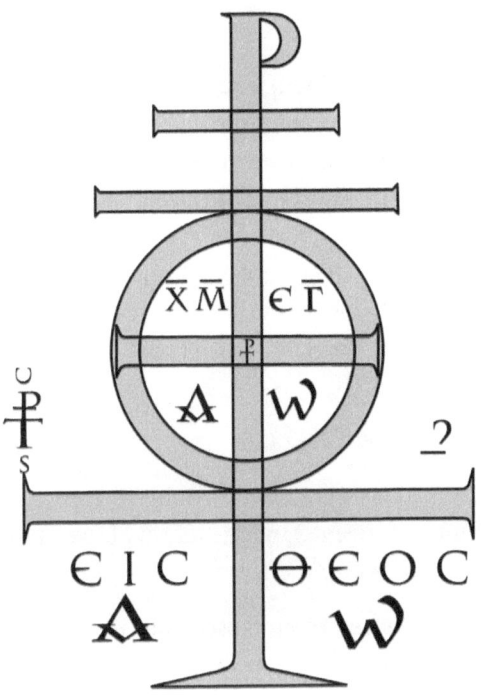

THE THREEFOLD OR TRIUNE BAPTISM

Taken from the Second Book of Jeu, what follows is the aforementioned Triune Baptism, adapted for use by the solitary practitioner in self-initiation as one of the "Sons of the Pleroma." It consists of a threefold baptism, by Water, by Fire, and by the Holy Spirit, each using a seal sacred and known unto the Master Yeshua.

The following rite is a working of astral magick, that is, magick to be carried out on the Astral Plane, either by way of conscious astral projection or by mental projection, if one has become sufficiently adept in the latter practice.

I. The Physical Temple

    a. The physical temple, or the room wherein you will begin the ceremony before entering the astral plane, is to be cleaned thoroughly prior to commencement.

    b. Let the magus beforehand ascertain which position, or asana, is most conducive to astral projection and/or the deepened state of meditation wherein mental projection is achieved for himself, and prepare the physical temple appropriately. Postures suggested for this astral working are lying prone or seated in the form of the Egyptian deities, however do not limit yourself to these. If another such position suits your will, let it be so.

II. The Astral Temple

    a. Before undertaking the rite proper, let the magus have established an astral temple down to the most minute of details, as are outlined in the rite, so that upon entrance it is as real to him as the room wherein he stands.

    b. The altar of the astral temple should be adorned with a white linen cloth upon which the Master shall place all the offerings.

III. Let the rite commence with the magus entering the physical temple and securing his space in the universe as suits his will and as befits the present working.

IV.   After the securing of space, let the magus take his place in the asana he has chosen, and establish a rhythmic breathing pattern of 7x7x7.[9]

V.   Once a state of relaxation sufficient for astral/ mental projection is reached, let this begin.

VI.   Once the magus has left the physical temple and entered the astral, let him be seated in the throne prepared for him.

VII.   While seated thus, let the magus observe the entry of the Master Yeshua, the teacher and initiator, who comes to stand before him. Let the magus rise and take to one knee, his left knee to the abyss and right the heavens, and above his head make the Coronastrum.

VIII.   The Master asks of the aspirant

What do you seek? What is your purpose?

IX.   To which the aspirant responds:

I seek the Threefold Baptism that I may enter the Treasury of Light and become a Son of the Pleroma.

X.   The Master says

Come forth and receive the three baptisms, and I will reveal to you the mystery of the Archons.

If my father so wills it, come forth and receive the Baptism of Water.

The Master places anemone flower in the aspirant's mouth, a sunflower plant in each of his hands, and places a loaf of bread and olive branches as an offering, thereafter circling the aspirant, stopping at each of the 4 corners of the world and at each proclaiming AMEN thrice, then returning to his place before the aspirant repeating AMEN thrice again, and invoking thus:

> *Hear me my father, thou father of all fatherhoods, thou infinite light who are in the treasury of light. May the parastatai come, they who serve the seven virgins of light*

---

9   That is, inhaling through the nose for a period of 7 seconds, holding the breath for 7 seconds, then slowly exhaling through the mouth for 7 seconds.

which are over the baptisms of life, whose unutterable names are these, ASTRAPA, TESPHOIODE, ONTIONOS, SINETOS, LACHON, PODITANIOS, OPAKIS, PHAEDROS, ODONTUCHOS, DIAKTIOS, KNESION, DROMIOS, EUIDETOS, POLYPAIDOS, and ENTROPON!

XI. The Master makes above the head of the seated aspirant the following sign and then continues:

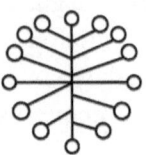

May they come and baptize my disciple in the baptism of Water, and the seven virgins of light forgive his sins and purify his iniquities and number him among the inheritors of the Kingdom of Light. If thou hast heard me, let now a sign be shown.

XII. The chalice of wine, previously to the right of the offerings, becomes water, into which the Master dips his finger, thereafter making this sign on the forehead of the aspirant

XIII. The Master proclaims

If my father so wills it, come forth and receive the Baptism of Fire.

The Master now adorns the white linen cloth with a censer in which burns holy incense, beside which lie vines of grape, juniper, myrrh, frankincense, mastic, and balsam. The Master again offers a loaf of bread and chalice of wine.

XIV. The Master places anemone flower in the aspirant's mouth and chrysanthemums in each of his hands, thereafter circling the aspirant and stopping at each of the 4 corners of the world , proclaiming AMEN thrice at each, and then returning to his place before the aspirant repeating AMEN thrice again, and invoking thus:

Hear me, my father, thou father of all fatherhoods, thou infinite light. Make my disciple worthy to receive the Baptism of Fire, and do thou forgive his sins and make him to be purified from his iniquities, those which he has committed knowingly and those which he has committed unknowingly, those he has committed from childhood until this day. Do thou cause Zorokothora Melchisedek to come in secret and bring the water of the baptism of Fire of the virgin of light, and the judge! I call upon thy imperishable names which are in the treasury of light,

AZARAKAZA AKA AMATHKRATITATH
YOYOYO
AMEN AMEN
YAOTH YAOTH YAOTH
PHAOPH PHAOPH PHAOPH
CHIOEPHOZPE CHENOBINUTH
ZARLAI LAZARLAI LAIZAI
AMEN AMEN AMEN
ZAZIZAUACH NEBEOUNISPH
PHAMOU PHAMOU PHAMOU
AMOUNAI AMOUNAI
AMEN AMEN AMEN
ZAZAZAZI ETAZAZA ZOTHAZAZAZ

XV.   The Master takes the censer of burning incense in his left hand, the grapevine in his right, and circles the magus thrice, counterclockwise, coming to a stop directly behind him. Raising the censer, he makes the following sign above the head of the aspirant

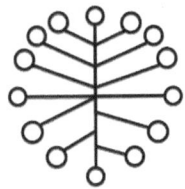

XVI.   In this moment the smoke of the incense takes the shape of this sacred seal, which the Master then makes in the ash on the forehead of his disciple

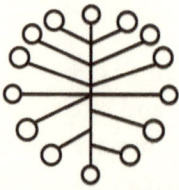

XVII.   The Master proclaims

Behold, you have received the Baptism of Water, and the Baptism of Fire, and now, if my father so wills it, I will give you the Baptism of the Holy Spirit.

XVIII. The Master makes an offering as before, with two chalices of wine, one on either side, a loaf of bread, branches of vine and juniper, saffron residue, cinnamon, myrrh, honey and balsam, and invokes:

Hear me, my father, father of all fatherhoods, thou infinite light, for I have called upon thy imperishable, unutterable names in the treasury of light. Forgive his sins and erase his iniquities and make him worthy to receive the Baptism of the Holy Spirit!

The Master now makes once again the sign,

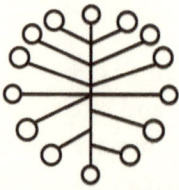

If thou hast heard me, and caused him to be numbered among the inheritors of the Kingdom of Light, Give me a sign!

XIX.   The sign having appeared thus, the Master then places it on the forehead of his disciple.

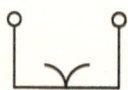

XX.   Let the aspirant now stand, having received the threefold baptism, placing his feet together, and proclaim the prayer:

Hear me, my father, father of all fatherhoods, thou infinite light, hear me and compel Sabaoth, the Adamas, and all his rulers to come and take from me all of my sins!

Whereafter the Master shall seal him with the following:

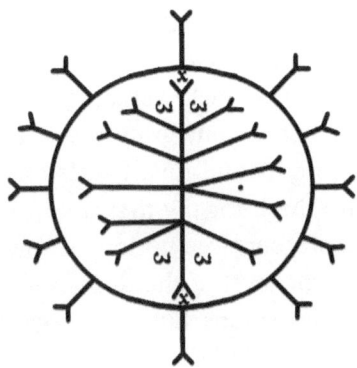

XXI.   Let the aspirant, now an initiate, circle to each of the corners of the world and repeat the previous prayer, after which the Master seals him with the Sign of Two Amens, which is:

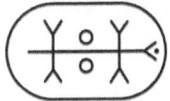

XXII.   Having thus received the threefold baptism, and having been sealed with the two holy and sacred seals of the father, the aspirant is now initiated in the mysteries and his magickal awakening commenced. Let him rise and re-enter his physical body, no longer a man but now a magus, and a follower of the Master Yeshua.

THE INVOCATION OF GABRIEL

The Archangel לְאִירְבַּג, Gabriel, unto whom the following working is dedicated, has the distinction of being named in both the Old and New Testament as well as the Quran, in addition to appearing in various other traditions throughout history, to include that of the "Latter Day Saints," the Gnostic works, Enoch, and the Coptic Christian magickal corpus from which this grimoire is derived.

Gabriel, like his sibling Michael, has long been regarded as being favorably disposed to the magus inclined to work with him, and I have found this to be true. My first work with Gabriel, excluding of course the minor role he plays in the Golden Dawn-style pentagram rites, came by way of the next rite, which while quite lengthy and involved, is one well worth the effort and work. Having been raised, for my first dozen years, in a "submarine Catholic"[10] family, I had preconceived notions as to Gabriel's character and status, relegating him to the level of the Roman Catholic saints to whom one prayed for various intercessions, but never regarding him as a being of great power. This was the case until I was introduced to the Books of Enoch wherein his *true* form was presented; in those works' description of him he is ruler over the Ikisat, the Seraphim, and Cherubim, and presiding over "all that is powerful."

It is in this capacity, as lord of all that is powerful, that we work with Gabriel in the rite that follows. It is imperative that the adjurations be spoken with the sincerity and respect one would pay the most revered of elders, for in my experience the one thing Gabriel will not brook is disrespect or condescension.

I.   The rite is to be commenced on Monday in the 3rd hour of the Moon and should be prefaced by a period of preparation as outlined in the beginning of this chapter, wherein internal and external purifications are observed and the utmost care is taken not to involve oneself in negative or counterproductive activities.

II. The temple is to be laid out with an image of the four holy archangels, that is to say Michael, Gabriel, Raphael, and Uriel placed in the center of the altar, with a white chime candle placed before each of

---

10   That is, a defunct Catholic family which appears or "surfaces" at church only twice a year(Christmas and Easter) thereafter disappearing again until the next of these holidays as do the submariners.

the four images. Atop the altar a censer in which burns frankincense, cinnamon, rose oil, and storax on charcoal made from wood. Underneath the censer, let the name of Gabriel be written in the blood[11] of the practitioner seeking to meet him.

III.   Let the rite commence with the Adjuration of Metatron, after which the magus takes his place behind the altar, and invokes thus:

> *I invoke thee, the one who governs from heaven to earth,*
> *From earth to heaven,*
> *The great self begotten one, whom begot only one;*
> *Give ear unto me, for I call to you!*
> *Only father, almighty father,*
> *The mind who art hidden in and of the father,*
> *The firstborn of every creature in every Aeon.*

IV.   Ignite the incense, circumambulate thrice counterclockwise, each time you arrive at the easternmost point proclaiming ABLANA-THANALBA (3x) and knocking thrice on the eastern wall.

V.   Continue the invocation:

> *Give ear unto me, for I call to you,*
> *The one who is over every Aeon,*
> *The firstborn of the first, in the names of all of the angels,*
> *Let them hear me, all of the angels and the archangels,*
> *Let them submit to me, all things of spiritual natures who are in this place!*
> *For this is the will of Sabaoth,*
> *Therefore help me, holy angels.*

VI.   Igniting the first candle, make above you the Coronastrum, and continue:

> *Michael, who is over all the strongest of powers,*
> *Raphael, who is over all of salvation,*

---

11   The original calls also for the sacrifice of 6 doves. The substitution of the magus' own blood is my own, and represents the way I have twice performed this rite successfully, having pricked the ring finger of my left hand to obtain a few drops and written he name of Gabriel in Hebrew therein. However for those squeamish about such things, it is worth mentioning that colleague of mine substituted "Dove's Blood" oil.

Gabriel, who is over the power,
Armael, who is over hearing,
Uriel, who is over the Crowns,
Nephael, who is over aid,
Akentael, who is over the stars,
Asentael, who is over the sun,
Eraphael, who is over the day,
Yeremiel, who is over the bowls of wrath,
Eriel, who is over the waters,
Phanuel, who is over the produce,
Aphael, who is over the snow,
Akrael, who is over the sea,
Meilael, who is over the rains,
Nabuel, who is over the skies,
Rathiel, who is over the plains,
Thauruel, who is over the clouds,
Abrasaxael, who is over the lightning,
Yaoel, who is over every place and all things,
Sabael, who is over the good among us,
Adonael, who is over the coming in and going forth of the father,
By all the Holy Angels, in their reign and kingdoms, Hear me!

VII. Lighting the second candle, continue:

Holy, Holy, Holy is the Lord, first father of fatherhoods,
Heaven and earth are full of his glory!
In his name do I invoke and glorify thee, Gabriel, who stand to
the left of the father,
I glorify you, Gabriel, by IAO in all his Holiness,
I glorify you, Gabriel, by the holy one Sabaoth, first of heaven
and earth,
I glorify you, Gabriel, by Adonai, and by Elohim, O thou first of
the Cherubim and Seraphim,
I glorify you, Gabriel, by Marmaraoth, who is before both angel
and archangel!
I glorify you, Gabriel, by Akrammachamari, who is before the
fourteen firmaments,

I glorify you Gabriel, by Thakrai, who has arrayed the earth upon the abyss, and the heaven as a vault
I glorify you, Gabriel, by Manachoth, who laid the foundations of heaven and of earth, and established the fourteen firmaments upon the four pillars
I glorify you, by Lauriel, the minister of your brother Raphael,
I glorify you, by the heavens and by the earth,
I glorify you, by the sun and by the moon,
I glorify you, by the stars and by the seas,

Hear me!
Come to me, O Gabriel!

VIII. Ignite the third candle, visualize the heavens above opening revealing a portal through which one may descend and enter the temple, and continue:

I adjure you today, O Gabriel, By Saber Blararo, and by the three presences which are in the midst of the four pillars that lift up heaven and earth; they are Thalamora, Thesoha and Thaisara!

I adjure you, O Gabriel, by the four angels who stand by the four pillars, whose feet set upon the foundations of the abyss, and by the three holy ones who lift up the heavens; they are Theriel, Throel and Bael!

I invoke you, four great angels before whom I stand! Come forth, O Gabriel, angel of righteousness, and reveal to me your glory!

IX. Ignite the fourth candle, and continue in the invocation:

I adjure you, Gabriel, by the four corners of the fourteen firmaments, that you come and be with me this day, and through your indescribable might educate me!

I adjure you, by your name Yoiriel, and by the cloud of light that is with the father, in which he was hidden before he created creation, whose name is Marmarami, the great palace of the spirit of Adonai, Elohim almighty!

Appear before me, O Gabriel, O angel of righteousness, and scatter before me all spirits of Satan and all of my enemies!

Lord God almighty, send unto me Gabriel, that he may come to me quickly!

AMEN (3x)

By your great name, IAO, SABAOTH, ADONAI, ELOHIM, almighty, I call to you, the greatest of gods who exists behind seven curtains, and who is seated upon his Holy throne, send to me Gabriel, who is over all powers, who is over the seraphim and the cherubim, holder of the trumpet of doom, with his sword unsheathed and in hand, that he may cast from me all unclean spirits, and that he may reveal to me the mystery of mysteries!

I invoke you by your honored names, ADONAI, ELOHIM, ELEMA, SABAKTANI, the one who gazes towards the heavens causing them to tremble, and before whom the very earth moves! By SABA SABAB SABAOTH, your secret name as the god who is seated in the heights.

I invoke you, Gabriel, by the head of Bathuriel, the great father, and by Orphamiel, the finger with which he grasps all of divinity! Descend to me Gabriel, whose secret name is ATHONATH, ATHONATH hear me!

X. It is at this point that Gabriel has arrived, on both occasions wherein I have used this rite to call upon him. The original, however, prescribes further invocation, which may indeed be used if Gabriel has not yet attended you, adjuring him in the names of yet other divinities:

I invoke you, O Gabriel,
By the great name of the father and to his glory
And by those who stand in his presence,
Athonas Siak Ksas Sabak Kaab, Kaesas Ekoe!

I invoke you, O Gabriel,
By the head of Michael, Raphael, Anlel, Sariel,
Auriel, Phariel, Sasael, Nechiel, Adoniel, Thrielm, Athiel and Akutael,
Who stand round the invisible father and his holy throne.

I invoke you, O Gabriel, By the seven archangels,
Tophou and Raphael, Bariel, Arthamiel, Arophtebel, Lanach,
Ephnix,
Who stand in the presence of the father, listening to the proceedings
of his mouth AMEN (7 times)

I invoke you, O Gabriel,
By the Holy names of the Father,
Marinab Marmarou Babam Phioou Bathuriel
IAO SABAOTH ADONAI PANCRATOR EMMANUEL
ABATHOU YACHAOI ICHAOF SABAOTH,
That you come to me here, in this place consecrated unto thee, by
virtue of all those in whose names I have invoked you.

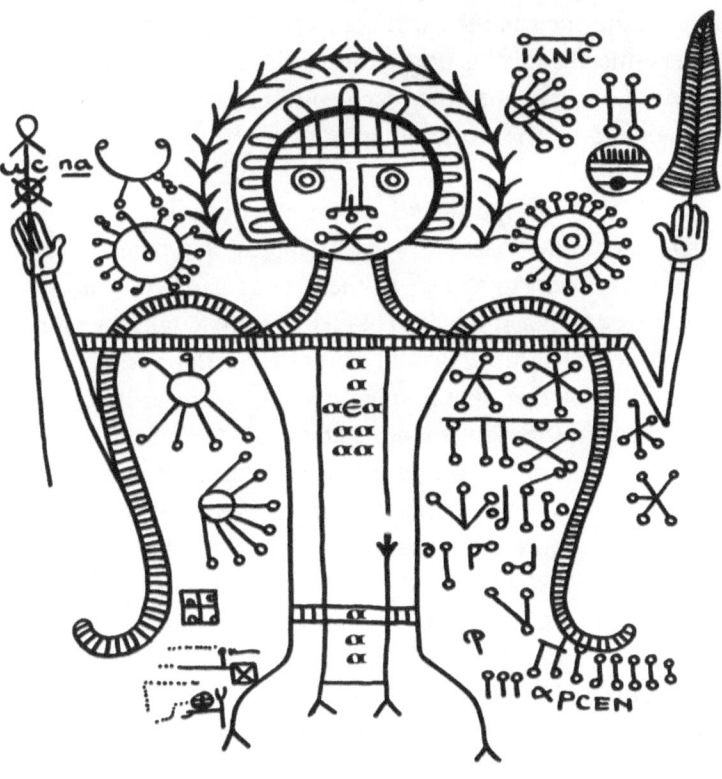

A NOTE ON THE APPEARANCE OF THE EVOKED

Before moving on, it would be valuable to touch briefly on the manner and likenesses in which those that we call on appear. This is necessary because, on two occasions, students with whom I have worked have come to me perplexed after execution of these rites of evocation; once with Gabriel, as just shared, as well as an evocation of Eleleth. The two aspiring evocators, while quite pleased with the arrival of "a spirit" in a form that was visible and not merely "perceived mentally," were reluctant to accept that the spirit who did appear was in fact he whom they called, since the manifestation was not in keeping with traditional depictions of them.

While it is possible for a mischievous or malignant entity to, having overheard your call to another or having been engaged in some nefarious deeds of his own, take advantage of your evoked's absence by appearing and posing as the one you seek, it is not likely. The phenomena which many practitioners mistake for this type of deception is quite often the stirring of restless dead, *Genii Loci* or other such spirits in response to the magickal current generated by the working, and not a real attempt by any devilish being to mislead you.

The fact is that the spirits with whom we work, be they demonic, celestial, angelic or otherwise, are wont to appear in whatever fashion they choose; charging them to appear in their true form serves no purpose as they have no true forms. If the likes of Eleleth were to take on a form appropriate to his celestial nature, it would dwarf the Earth on which it stood. The magus will find, however, that frequently the gods, regardless of their pantheon, do appear in the countenance traditionally ascribed to them. This is not because it is their only form, or even their actual one, but rather because it is that with which man has come to identify them and in which they will be recognized. Therefore the appearance of an attending spirit should never be the sole factor by which we judge their identity, regardless of whether it appears before you visibly or in a medium such as a crystal or mirror.

Likewise, the time when it was necessary to adjure a demon not to appear in a horrific or frightening form has long since past. We are of a generation which has given faces and personalities to the worst of our terrors in movies and every aspect of our culture in the form of *Saw*, *Candyman* and other Hollywood horrors, projecting the worst of our fears onto the screen. The arrival of a spirit "bellowing, with the body of a lion and head of an ass," is no longer the terrible sight it would have been to our predecessors (who would surely find the villains in our movies far more terrifying-looking than Agares).

What follows next may be recognized by the reader, as portions of it are drawn from one of the more widely-known rites of the PGM. Indeed a small part of this working forms the tail-end of one of the rites introduced in the chapter on the securing of one's space, further demonstrating the versatility of the system. As presented herein, it is a 7-day working in which each day the practitioner invokes the deity of the governing planet. The invocation finds its roots in "The Eighth Book of Moses," (or PGM XIII) yet it has been greatly expanded from the original in order to better accomplish what I set forth to do.

In its root form this invocation serves as an initiation for the aspirant, wherein he calls on both Helios and Aion, intoning a plethora of divine names or *voces magicae* purported to be Birdglyphic, Baboonic and more, and entreats them to affect his magickal transformation. In the variant provided below, the same two transcendent deities are called upon to facilitate the practitioner's invocation of their counterparts on each of their respective days.

Among the materia necessary for completion of this rite are the "seven secret incenses" spoken of in the Eighth Book of Moses:

1. The proper incense of Kronos is storax, for it is heavy and fragrant

2. Of Zeus: malabathron[12]

3. Of Ares: kostos

4. Of Helios: frankincense

5. Of Aphrodite: Indian nard

6. Of Hermes: cassia

7. Of Selene: myrrh

Each to be sacrificed on the appropriate day alongside "the flowers of the 7 stars," which are marjoram, white lily, lotus, erephyllinon, narcissus, gillyflower, and rose, dried, ground into powder and used with the incense of the day for suffumigation.

---

12   Μαλαβάθρον, or Indian Bay-Leaves

The rite is to be commenced on Sunday, in the third of the hours ruled by Helios. We begin the 7-day working thus because it is by the entreaty to Helios and procurement of his blessings in the endeavor that we will thereafter seek to invoke those that follow. As with the previous working, it is recommended that the practitioner devote 3 days prior to this rite for preparation, fasting, and purification.

I.   Sunday, in the third hour of the Sun, enter the temple and stand before the altar, atop which is the censer with the incense appropriate to the day and the flowers of the seven stars.

II.   Open the ceremony by utilization of steps 1-9 in "The Calling of the Sevenths," ceasing after step 9.

III.   Begin the preliminary invocation thus:

I call upon you, who are greater than all, the creator of all, you, the self-begotten, who see all and are not seen; for you gave Helios the glory and all the power, Selene the privilege to wax and wane and have fixed courses, yet you took nothing from the earlier-born darkness, but apportioned things so that they would be equal; for when you appeared, both order arose and light appeared. All things are subject to you, whose true form none of the gods can see; who can change into all forms. You are invisible, Aion of aions!

I call upon you, eternal and unbegotten, who are one, who alone holds together the whole of creation, whom none understands, whom the gods worship, whose name not even the gods can utter.

IV.   Ignite the incense, circumambulate thrice counterclockwise while invoking:

Create a vortex of energy, quickly. I call on your name, the greatest among gods. Open, open, four quarters of the cosmos, for the lord of the inhabited world comes forth. Archangels, decans, angels rejoice, for Aion of aions himself, the only transcendent, invisible, AION OF AION, goes through this place. By the name AIA AINRUKATH[13], cast up, earth, for the lord, all things you

---

13   AIA AINPYXAΘ

contain, for he is the storm-sender and controller of the abyss, master of fire!

Grant, O God, That I may be initiated into the mysteries of HELIOS, of AHEBUKROM!

V.   Once again, take thy place behind the altar. Visualize the opening of the 7 portals, and invoke Helios thus:

Come to me, Thou from the four winds, ruler of all, who breathed spirit into men for life, whose is the hidden and unspeakable Name – it cannot be uttered by human mouth and at whose Name even the daimons, when hearing, are terrified; whose is the Sun, ARNEBOUAT BOLLOKH BARBARIKH BAALSAMĒM PTIDAIOU ARNEBOUAT, and the Moon, ARSENPENPRŌOUTH BARBARAIŌNE OSRAR MEMPSEKHEI – they are unwearied eyes shining in the pupils of men's eyes – of whom heaven is head, ether body, earth feet, and the environment water, the Agathos Daimon. Thou art the ocean, begetter of good things and feeder of the civilized world. Thine is the eternal processional way in which Thy seven-lettered Name is established

for the harmony of the seven sounds of the planets, which utter their voices according to the 28 forms of the Moon: SAR APHARA APHARA I ABRAARM ARAPHA ABRAAKH PERTAŌMĒKH AKMĒKH IAŌ OUE Ē IAŌ OUE EIOU AEŌ EĒOU IAŌ. Thine are the beneficent rays of the stars, daimons, Fortunes and Fates, by whom is given wealth, good old age, good children, good luck, and a good burial. And Thou, Lord of Life, King of the Heavens and the Earth and all things living in them, Thou whose justice is not turned aside, Thou whose glorious Name the muses sing, Thou whom the eight guards attend, Ē-Ō-KHŌ-KHOUKH-NOUN-NAUNIAMOUN-AMAUNI. Thou, who hast truth that never lies. Thy Name and Thy spirit rest upon the good. Come into my mind and my understanding for all the time of my life and accomplish for me all the desires of my soul.

For Thou art I, and I, Thee. Whatever I say must happen, for I have Thy Name as a unique phylactery in my heart, and no flesh, although moved, will overpower me; no spirit will stand against me – neither daimon nor visitation nor any other of the evil beings of Hades, because of Thy Name, which I have in my soul and invoke. Also be with me always for good, a good God dwelling on a good man, Thyself immune to magick, giving me health no magick can harm, well being, prosperity, glory, victory, power, sex appeal. Restrain the evil eyes of each and all of my legal opponents, whether men or women, but give me assistance in everything I do. ANOKH AIEPHE SAKTIETĒ BIBIOU BIBIOU SPHĒ SPHĒ NOUSI NOUSI SEĒE SEĒE SIETHŌ SIETHŌ OUN KHOUNTIAI SEMBI IMENOUAI BAINPNOUN PNOUTH TOUKHAR SOUKHAR SABAKHAR ANA IEOU ION EON THŌTH-Ō OUTHRO THRŌRESE ERIŌPŌ IUĒ AĒ IAŌAI AEĒIOUŌ AEĒIOUŌ ĒOKH MANEBI KHUKHIŌ ALARAŌ KOL KOL KAATŌN KOLKANTHŌ BALALAKH ABLALAKH OSERKHENTHE MENTHEI BOULŌKH BOULŌKH OSERKHENTE MENTHEI,

I have received the power of Abraham, Isaac and Jacob, and of the great God, daimon IAŌ ABLANATHANALBA SIABRATHILAŌ LAMPSOUTĒR IĒI ŌŌ, God. Lord PERTAŌMĒKH

KHAKHMĒKH IAŌ OUĒE IAŌ OUĒE IEOU AĒŌ EĒOU IAŌ.

VI.   Having performed the preliminary invocation wherein Aion, and through him Helios are summoned, provide now a statement of will that the Gods may know of your desire.[14]

VII.   Following the statement of intent, invoke thus:

I call Thee Lord, to cause to appear unto me the God _____109[15] in a good form, for under Thine order I serve Thine angel, BIATHIARBAR BERBIR EKHILATOUR BOUPHROUMTRŌM, and Thy fear, DANOUP KHRATOR BELBALI BALBITH IAŌ. Through Thee arose the celestial pole and the earth. I call Thee

---

14   An example thereof would be, "Grant, O Lord, Flawless, whom pollutes no place, that in this night I may become known unto thy son Ares, that by him my invocation may be heeded and that he may attend me" (using, of course, the name of the deity to whom the day belongs).

15   Here inserting the name of the invoked.

lord, as do the Gods who appeared under Thine order, that they may have power, ACHEBUKRON, who is Helios, to whom belongs the glory, AAA ĒĒĒ ŌŌŌ III AAA ŌŌŌ SABAŌTH ARBATHIAŌ ZAGOURĒ, the god ARATHU ADONAI.

I call on thee lord, in 'birdglyphic', ARAI; in hieroglyphic, LAILAM; in Hebrew, ANOK BIATHIARBATH BERBIR EKHILATOUR BOUPHROUMTRŌM; in Egyptian, ALDABAEIM; in baboonic, ABRASAX; in falconic, KHI KHI KHI KHI KHI KHI KHI TIPH TIPH TIPH; in hieratic, MENEPHŌIPHŌTH KHA KHA KHA KHA KHA KHA KHA.

VIII.   Immediately following this invocation, clap thy hands thrice, intone loudly POP POP POP, and make, for a space of seven seconds, the sound of the serpent.[16]

IX.   Having invoked by these means the deity who governs the day, honor them by way of the appropriate Orphic Hymn, and by adding to the incense more of the blend sacred to him/her.

X.   Following the whole of this ceremony, let the temple be closed.

This ceremony, as aforementioned, is to be repeated daily for each of seven days, the last of which will be on Saturday in the hour of Kronos, for as it is said in the papyri, "Old Kronos, a defeated god yet one powerful, should be met only when the blessings of all his children are yours."

The ceremony itself remains the same, save for the substitution of the day's ruling deity for that of the previous and use of the correct incense and Orphic Hymn. Therefore we will not herein present the full text of each day's rite, instead trusting that one who has progressed far enough to contemplate undertaking this work will not neglect to make all such substitutions prior to commencement of each day's portion.

---

16   That is to say, *hiss.*

ASCENSION THROUGH THE HEAVENS

The second of the two promised rites from Bruce Codex is another working of Astral Magick, and one that demonstrates clearly that the practitioners of that age valued such astral operations greatly.

The rite of Ascent through the Heavens furthers the initiatory awakening commenced with the Triune Baptism, now bringing the initiate into direct contact with the rulers of the heavens by way of the astral plane. Having received the baptisms of water, of the Holy Spirit, and of fire, and by virtue of the sacred seals given him by the Master, the initiate is now received by each of the rulers in turn and given admittance to their realm.

Outwardly, and at first glance, this rite is a very long and involved one, and yet one which is obviously of great significance. I caution the reader not to allow himself for a moment to consider that the outer and immediately evident virtue of this working is the limit thereof, for this single rite and those that surround it in the Bruce Codex contain mysteries within enigmas which have been wrapped in secrets and thereafter veiled. Indeed the rites in this Codex, properly understood, represent a lifetime of magickal work and learning.

I. The rite is to commence on Sunday, the practitioner having spent the previous three days in preparation as prescribed previously.

II. The physical temple is to be laid out identically as it was in the rite of the Triune Baptism. Repeating for convenience sake:

   a. The physical temple, or the room wherein you will begin the ceremony before entering the Astral Plane, is to be cleaned thoroughly prior to commencement.

   b. Let the magus beforehand ascertain which position, or asana, is most conducive to astral projection and/or the deepened state of meditation wherein mental projection is achieved for himself, and prepare the physical temple appropriately. Postures suggested for this astral working are lying prone or seated in the form of the Egyptian Deities, however do not limit yourself to these. If another such position suits your will, let it be so.

III. The astral temple should be akin to a Greek temple, over top of which shines the Sun in all its radiance. Within are marbled floors, and an ever-burning fire behind which is an altar. Atop the altar a censer, burning the sacred incense. The whole of the temple is alight only by the rays of the sun. The Master sits, enthroned, behind the altar. Before him a pillow atop which the initiate will sit.

IV.   Let the rite commence with the magus entering the physical temple and securing his space in the universe as suits his will and as befits the present working.

V.   After the securing of space, let the magus take his place in the asana he has chosen, and establish a rhythmic breathing pattern of 7x7x7.[17]

VI.   Once a state of relaxation sufficient for astral/mental projection is reached, let this begin.

VII.   Once the magus has left the physical temple and entered the astral, let him be seated at the foot of the Master on the pillow prepared for him.

VIII.   Once before the Master Yeshua, let the initiate take to one knee, his left knee to the abyss and right the heavens, and above his head make the Coronastrum.

IX.   The Master thereafter returns the sign, and bids his student sit.

X.   Seated upon the pillow, let the initiate proclaim:

My lord, my teacher, I beg thee that thou shouldst place in me the mystery of the forgiveness of sins, and its defences, and its seal, so that I may become the son of the light, and so the archons of the aeons which guard the treasury of the light do not seek to restrain me, and so that I may be numbered within the inheritors of the Kingdom of Light, and be initiated in all of the mysteries of the father of all fatherhoods!

XI.   The Master rises from his throne, nods his assent and speaks:

Be patient, my son, and I will teach you this mystery of mysteries, open the gates of the aeons. Hear now, since you have received the mystery of the 12 aeons, and the baptism of the water of life, and

---

17   That is, inhaling through the nose for a period of 7 seconds, holding the breath for 7 seconds, then slowly exhaling through the mouth for 7 seconds.

the mystery of the baptism of fire, and the mystery of the Holy Spirit. So too shall you now know the mystery of the defenses to evil, and gain welcome in the heavens.

Take thou my hand, and rise through the planes. When you come forth from the body and reach the first aeon, when the archons thereof accost you, seal yourself with this seal, the cipher of which is 1119.

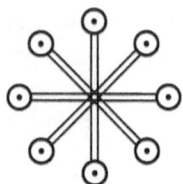

Proclaim before the archons "Withdraw yourselves, you archons of the first aeon, for I call upon JEU, whose name I know!" Whereafter, upon hearing this name, the archons will be afraid and flee to the west, allowing you to rise through the first heaven.

XII. As the initiate ascends and rises through the first heaven, reaching the gate of the second, the Master instructs further

When you come forth from the body and reach the second aeon, when the archons thereof accost you, seal yourself with this seal, the cipher of which is 2219.

Proclaim before the archons, "Withdraw yourselves, you archons of the second aeon, for I call upon JEU, whose name I know!" Whereafter, upon hearing this name, the archons will be afraid and flee to the west, allowing you to rise through the second heaven.

XIII.   Continuing in his ascent, passing through the second heaven, the initiate is instructed:

When you reach the third aeon, the realm of IALDABAOTH, who himself will come forth to restrain you from passing above him, seal thyself with this seal, the cipher of which is 3349.

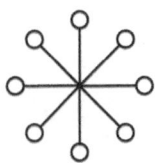

Command, then, in the name of JEU, "IALDABAOTH! Withdraw thyself and thy archons, for I seek JEU, who is the father of fatherhoods!"

XIV.   Rising above the angered Ialdabaoth, enraged but powerless to restrain you, ascend further until you reach the gate of the fourth heaven, that which is governed by SAMAELO.

When you reach the fourth aeon, who is SAMAELO, seal thyself with this seal, the cipher of which is 4555.

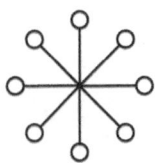

When SAMAELO or his archons approach, proclaim "SAMAELO! As thou canst restrain me, for I come in the name of JEU, restrain thy archons and withdraw!"

Whereafter they will be greatly afraid and will flee to the west, whilst you rise on.

XV.   Rising yet higher, ascending through the limits of the heaven of the aeon SAMAELO, stand thou before the gate of the fifth aeon, hear the words of the Master:

When you reach the gate of the fifth aeon and when cometh the archons thereof, seal thyself with this seal, the cipher of which is 5369.

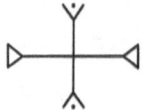

Command, "Ye archons of the fifth aeon, retreat! Withdraw! For JEU commands it!"

XVI.   Ascend! Rise thou further, to the 6th heaven its gate, and be not befuddled by the pleasantness of those that you find therein! Be not deterred, yea rise and ascend!

When you reach the 6th heaven, that which is called the "Little Midst", for therein the archons have yet a little goodness within them, seal thyself with this seal, the cipher of which is 6915, and bid them farewell.

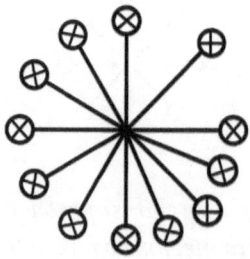

Proclaim, "Withdraw, ye archons of The Little Midst, for by JEU I have received the mystery of the twelve aeons and their defences," whereupon they will immediately make way for you and rejoice for you with great joy.

XVII.   Rise thou to the seventh aeon, sealing thyself with the next seal, that of the seventh heaven, the cipher of which is 7889.

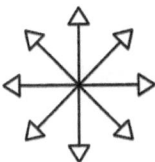

Waste not thy time here, but command these archons in the name of JEU, causing their retreat.

XVIII.   Reaching the 8th aeon, repeat thou the sealing using the seal the cipher of which is 8054

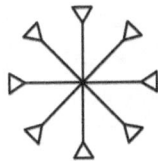

And thereafter banish the archons and rise thou further.

XIX.   The seal of the 9th aeon has a cipher which is 2889, and is made thus

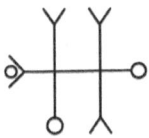

Seal thyself therewith, command the archons thereof and rise thou to the heaven the tenth.

XX.   Reaching the tenth aeon, seal thyself with the seal

The cipher of which is 4559.

XXI. The seal by which the initiate gains passage through the 11th heaven, or aeon, has a cipher which is 5558, and which appears thusly

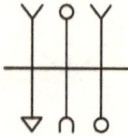

XXII. Ascend once more, finally reaching the twelfth high heaven, hear the voice of the Master yet again:

Know that the invisible God is in this place with Barbelo, and is the unbegotten God. The unbegotten God is in a place alone in this 12th heaven, and the veils are drawn before him. For there are many other gods in this place which is The Treasury of Light, and they are called archons. They are the great archons who rule over all the aeons, and it is they who serve the invisible God, Barbelo, and the unbegotten one.

Seal thyself before the face of the unbegotten God, using the holy seal which is

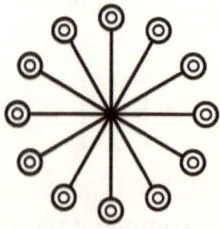

The cipher of this seal is 9885, and contains a great mystery of itself.

XXIII. Having sealed himself thus, the initiate is approached and applauded by "The 24 emanations of the invisible God" because "they envy you because of these mysteries you have received, and they shall want to take hold of you, to hold you." Show them the Seal of 8855, which is

XXIV. Having sealed thyself with the seal of which the cipher is 8855, let the initiate proceed now before the throne of the invisible God, Barbelo, the unbegotten one and bask in the glory of the father of all fatherhoods. The sun surmounts his temple and sits within, for he keeps it ever alight.

THE INVOCATION OF ABRASAX

Abrasax being the god for whom this tome was named, and indeed He who inspired its creation, it is only fitting that the final act of magick presented herein is the Invocation of Abrasax of which I availed myself in making initial contact with Him.

The Invocation of Abrasax provides a unique opportunity for the magus to form an intimate and lasting bond with the God, more so than would an evocation, as the result of the successful performance of this rite is spiritual, corporeal, and conscious union with Abrasax: wherein the God is brought to manifestation not in the physical world, but in the body of the invocator. It is our goal here to bring, if for a fleeting moment, a god not to us, but within us.

Before proceeding with the ritual proper, it befits me to spend a brief moment in explication of what is meant by "invocation" of Abrasax, and how it differs from the earlier evocations.

While the multitude of New Age and pseudo-magickal groups predominant in the modern day claim "invocation" as a core practice in their traditions, I have only infrequently found a practitioner whose "successful" experiences thereof indeed resulted in the invoked descending and indwelling them. Unlike in the practice of evocation, invocation lends itself to self-delusion in that success therein can be imagined with ease. A practitioner, in the throes of ecstatic ritual and the altered state of mind that comes with, can easily and innocently become fully convinced that he has indeed succeeded in an invocation, judging the bliss that often comes from magickal work as union with the invoked entity.

True invocation, wherein one opens a portal to our reality not in a magickal circle or shewstone, but within himself for a higher being to descend and indwell his body, is – to put it simply – possession. You concede control of your body and consciousness momentarily to the invoked, allowing them to partake of our world in fully physical form, albeit a borrowed one. Such an experience cannot fail to leave a permanent mark on the magus; not on the body where it can be seen, but on the psyche and on the soul. Therein lies the benefit and also the danger. While evocation, by comparison, ends with the departure of the spirit, invocation knows only a beginning, not an end.

This is the origin of the age-old axiom that we must "invoke" only the holy and divine entities and limit interaction with "demons" to evocation, lest the trauma of sharing ones being with such an evil entity leave him scarred mentally at best, and catatonic at worst. While I do not hold with this, simply because most of those entities regarded as "demons" are in fact deities whose only "evil" act is not being the God of Judeo-Christian society, I do caution any would-be invocator to investigate thoroughly the nature of any entity with whom he would share his body and consciousness. While the universe is populated by far fewer "evil" entities than mainstream religion would have you believe, it is not devoid of such beings. I have borne witness to the consequences of a practitioner opening herself to such a one, and it is a dread fate indeed.[1]

Therefore before concluding this brief digression on the natures of invocation and evocation, I again warn the aspiring invocator to know well all those whom he would invoke. Just as you would take pains to assure a person's good repute prior to giving them a room in your home, so should you practice even greater diligence when inviting one more powerful than him into your mind.

Returning now to the Invocation of Abrasax:

The rite itself is an amalgamation of several others scattered throughout the Coptic and Gnostic traditions, brought together as multiple pieces of a single puzzle, the sum of which is infinitely greater than its parts. During my initial foray into the magicks contained herein, the specific verses of which this rite makes use, and the order in which they appear, were provided to me as the means "by which the magus, sufficiently learned, could infallibly cause his call to be heard by Abrasax." As will be seen, a number of the magickal formulae and "Words of Power" found throughout the corpus are used herein, in a specific order, which must not be deviated from.

The rite which follows is to be commenced on Sunday, and in the second of the hours governed by the Sun, with the period of preparation having begun on the Sunday immediately prior.[2]

The rite requires very little in the way of materia. A single white candle, anointed with virgin olive oil or Abramelin Oil[3], a censer wherein offerings of frankincense and myrrh or Abramelin Incense are burned, A chalice of

---

1   Soror Lyric, who attempted an invocation of a spirit of Sumerian origin. After several days of clinical catatonia at Bellevue Hospital, spent yet another week re-learning how to talk, and who even now, two years later, has yet to regain about half of her mental capacity.
2   Unlike the preceding rites for which only 3 days preparation are indicated, the invocation of Abrasax must be prefaced by a 7 day purification and preparatory period.
3   German formula.

white wine, and an Abrasax Stone[4] should grace the altar, which is covered by a virgin white cloth.

In addition to the standard preparations presented elsewhere in this book, the means of preparing oneself for this rite specifically are as follows, and should be followed as diligently as possible.

DAY 1 – SUNDAY, DURING THE 2ND HOUR OF THE SUN.

- Clean the whole of the temple using an appropriate soap.[5]

- With Abramelin Oil, make on each of the four walls the following seal:

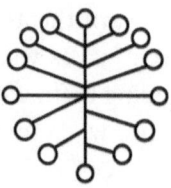

- Sitting in the center, with incense burning atop the altar, take the Abrasax Stone in thy left hand and methodically chant the name of ABRASAX, 365 times.

DAYS 2-4 –

- Repeat the exercise as above twice daily, chanting the name of the god 365 times in full whilst holding the stone or amulet.

DAY 5 & 6 –

- Repeat the exercise as above thrice daily, however chanting now the sacred name ABRASAX ABRASICHOU.

---

4   See examples thereof earlier in this work. The Abrasax talismans/amulets are equally suitable.
5   Florida Water, Sandalwood, etc.

DAY 7 - SATURDAY

- Repeat the prior day's chant (ABRASAX ABRASICHOU, 365 times) seven times throughout the day.

- After each 365th repetition, pray earnestly the following conjuration:

  O Great God Abrasax, One With The Glory Like Unto God, Come! In the name of the First of whom you are the Second, Come! Come, for I have said your signs and your seals that you may hear me!

DAY 8 – THE RITE PROPER

Commencing again in the 2nd of the solar hours, having spent the week prior in preparation, and in building about thyself the light of the God, begin the invocation.

THE INVOCATION OF ABRASAX

I.   Open the rite with the Calling of the Sevenths, whereafter the magus strikes a battery thrice three upon the altar top, after which he shall imperiously vibrate the name of the God, ABRASAX, 5 times.

II. Let the ceremony commence with the ignition of the candle and incense.

III. Let the magus take in his right hand the Abrasax Stone, raising above his head, and begin the invocation:

I call upon you,
who rules over the kingdom of power,
whose word is an offspring of light,
whose words are immortal,
eternal, immutable,
by whose will life is produced for all of creation,
whose word alone gives form to substance,
by whom the souls of man, of the archons and the angels are
moved...,
whose word reaches all of existence,
who has divided the eternal realm among the angels thereof,
who has created everything,
the invisible god one speaks to only in silence,

ZOXATHAZO
A
OOEE
OOO EEE
OOOO EE
OOOOOO OOOOO
OOOOOO UUUUUU
OOOOOOOOOOOOOOO
ZOZAZOTH

IV. Let the magus recite the name of the god, ABRASAX, 120 times, vibrating from deep within.

V.   Lowering your hand to the level of your heart, continue:

Descend now, thou who hast a name for each day in the year,
the sum of whose name is 365, verily, come, and appear, in the
name of IAO[6]
I have called upon the name of my Father, so that he should
move thee, in order that you may emanate and come forth!
In the name of IAO, come thou forth and indwell my soul,
ABRASAX, whose hand stretches out over the rays of Helios!
Yea, for I adjure you by the power of Chabarach Rinischir
Phunero Phontel Asoumar Asoumar,
who enlighten the underworld in the evening
and the earth in the morning.
You must give me the sun as a garment,
the moon with which I cover myself' as a cloak!

VI.   Let the magus recite the name of the god, ABRASAX, 120 times in the manner as before.

VII.   Continue the invocation:

Come, O merciful god of the aeon, who has ascended to the
seventh heaven, who has come from the right of the father,

AEEIOUO
AEEIOU
AEEIO
AEEI
AEE
AE
A

I invoke you, ABRASAX,
Lord of whole earth and the heavens!
I invoke you, O great one, the second of the first,
Whose are the restraints with which the abyss is bound!
I invoke you, O God of the Sun,
Whom Helios reveres!
Descend! Endacare!,

---

6   "JEU," as in the Books of Jeu from the Bruce Codex, who is IAO to other Gnostic sects.

Let my breath be the breath of thy lungs,
Let me speak with thy voice!

VIII.   Let the magus vibrate 120 times the name of the god.

IX.   Let the invocation reach its culmination:

HAPEHIPAHAU HAELEC NAMAROUTHINIA (repeat three tmes)

AKASHTHINIA MOUNTHARAHA MATHIROTHA (repeat six times)

EIA EIAAK MIAAK SEMIAAK ARTORE ARTORAN NARTORAK (repeat five times)

Come, ABRASAX, Come!

X.   If ABRASAX has, by this point, come, there will be no further conscious effort on the part of the magus, as the remainder of the ceremony will be carried out by him. If, however, he has yet to descend, the following invocation, which we have shared earlier in this work, may be applied here in replication:

I adjure you by your powers, your names,
By your holy potencies;
I adjure you by Orphamiel
the great finger of the father
I adjure you by the throne of the father
I adjure you by Orpha,
the entire body of god;
I adjure you by the chariots of the sun;
I adjure you by the entire host of angels on high;
I adjure you by the seven curtains that are drawn over the
face of god
I adjure you by the seven cherubim who fan the face
of god;
I adjure you by the great cherub of fire, whose name no
one knows;
I adjure you by the great name of god, whose name no
one knows except the camel!

ABLANNATHANABLAN
ABLANNATHANABLA
ABLANNATHANABL
ABLANNATHANAB
ABLANNATHANA
ABLANNATHAN
ABLANNATHA
ABLANNATH
ABLANNA
ABLANN
ABLAN
ABLA
ABL
AB
A

XI.   The god having come, he will reveal to you his heart-seal, which is his 365th name, a name consisting of 365 Greek letters, which can nonetheless be pronounced perfectly in any known language.[7]

XII.   If ABRASAX has yet to arrive, pursuing the invocation further will not be advantageous at this point. If the Will of the magus is strong enough, he may recommence the following day, beginning from Step I of the invocation proper, else he may take pause and abandon the rite until a future time.

---

7   "Allegedly." I, however, have transliterated it into only 6, though it can indeed be pronounced perfectly in each of them.

THE RECEIVED WISDOM OF THE GOD ABRASAX, *IN PARABOLAM*

The word "parable" comes from the Greek παραβολή (parabolē), meaning "comparison, illustration, analogy." A parable is a succinct story, in prose or verse, which illustrates one or more instructive principles, or lessons.[8]

---

8   Wikipedia

I.

...The student then approached the Magus, and earnestly said, "Brother, as much as I want to learn, and as much I want to succeed, as much as I study and practice, why can I not advance? Why has my ascension become stagnant?"

To which the Magus replied, "When you truly want to succeed, you will. You do not yet want it."

Befuddled, the aspirant replied, "But I do! I do want it, I do want to be like you!"

The Magus considered the aspirant briefly and then said "if this is true, if your desire is real and your want of this magical art is genuine, follow me."

Leading his pupil to the banks of the Nile, the Magus instructed the student to enter therein and bathe, that he may be cleansed. Following his teacher's instruction, the aspirant did so, whereupon the Magus seized the back of his student's head and forced him underwater, holding him there and allowing him no room for escape. The student fought, kicking, his arms flying wildly about with the strength of a man in whom the instinct for survival has taken over, and though he was but a boy and physically diminutive, his efforts were rewarded when he succeeded in pushing the teacher from him, rising and taking a breath at the last moment before his lungs filled with water and took from him his life.

Now afloat, gasping to fill his aching lungs with the precious air he so fought for, the student attempted to stand, exhausted and utterly without energy, every muscle in his body protesting the intense exertion through which they had been put. His teacher came to his side and lifted him to his feet. Bewildered at his teacher's having attempted to kill him only to thereafter help him, the aspirant nonetheless accepted his aid.

Upon reaching the shore, the Magus asked of the aspirant, "In that moment, underwater, helpless, and certain of your impending death, why did you fight me? Why did you resist?"

To which the young man replied, "I was near to death! Why do you imagine I fought you, madman! My only thought was of my need for air, my only desire was a single breath! I wanted to breathe!"

The Magus then smiled, and replied, "When your desire to succeed in your magical art is equal to your desire for that breath, you will have your success."

II.

"Teacher?" said the student, now an adept in his own right.

"Yes my son?" responded the Magus.

"Master, long have I studied under you, and much have I learned. I entered your tutelage a naïve child, seduced by the prospect of worldly power and wealth, and you brought me forth a man who has stood before the gods themselves, a man who wields the crook and staff of the magus. All that I sought when I came to you I have found, and more. Yet now there exists a question for which I can form no answer."

The Master replied, "And what is it that troubles you son? Have I been derelict in my instruction? What have I neglected to teach you?"

Taken aback and not wanting to offend his teacher, the student said "No, lord, you have in no way been negligent in your instruction. More than I could ever have imagined you have imparted. And yet while you have given to me freely of your wisdom, your theories and the techniques with which our magick is made, never have you entrusted to me the mechanisms by which our magick works. Never have you shared with me the universal laws governing the legions of angels and demons by which they are placed at our call. So much I have learned, so much I have done! I stand before gods, known only to others in prayer, and from them receive instruction, and yet I know not how come they to exist. The universal truths and divine mandates which set it all into motion are alien to me, for never have you shed light on them. Would that you could divulge such gems of wisdom to me, I find that I would have completed a journey, having learned the truth of creation and the means by which the whole of the universe is given form. My wish, my lord, is to know that which is known of the first father, the divine mind behind all that you have shown me and all that I have beheld."

Deep within the Magus welled a satisfaction that never before had he felt. For the whole of his life he had awaited a student who would, at the twilight of his apprenticeship, come forth with this question. The Magus replied, "My son, far have you surpassed all of my other students in your ascent and comprehension of all that I have imparted, and wise far beyond your years have you become. Now, in my 84th year, at the dawn of my life and as I prepare to cross the river and stand before the measurer of hearts and judge of men, I will make you my heir. All that is mine I will give to you. For like you, I once asked this question of my own teacher. As do you in this moment, I sought those universal truths. … In all the religions of man I found tales of the first father, of his creation of all that is, and the governance of the whole of that creation, and yet no two were alike. Seeking to know the truth of the matter, and to know therefore the mechanisms by which our magick works while also the magick of others who rely onother gods do work, I asked my teacher to share with me this knowledge.

"When I made this request of my teacher, that he share with me the truth of creation, the identity of the creator and the laws by which magick works, by which it is governed and which give it life, he deigned to grant my entreaty. My master in that day entrusted to me a journal which had been passed down to him by his own teacher, who received it from the master who instructed him in this art, and so on it went. My teacher told me that this memoir had been begun before the stones which now form the pyramid before which you kneel were torn from the earth, and that each master had been instructed to pass it on to their spiritual heir as they prepare to make the great journey. Within this journal, each of us in whose care it has been placed has recorded all that we have learned which is absolute and unchanging. All the universal truths that can be known and all of the divine laws revealed to us, all the certainties with regard to the divine mind and the powers by which our magick is accomplished are recorded herein.

"Because you, my son, have earned this right; I entrust this tome to you, that as have all we who preceded you, you too may record all the absolute truths of magick to which you are made privy, that the circle begun all those years ago may remain unbroken."

The pages which follow represent a complete and faithful reproduction of the journal as delivered by the master unto his student.

THE BOOK OF ABSOLUTES

Being the record of all of which the magus can be assured, wherein are presented all of the certainties, immutable laws and absolute ordinances with regard to the Sacred Art of Magick, and representing an accurate depiction of all aspects of divine magick which remain static and unassailable.

Fin.

BIBLIOGRAPHY

TEXTS

Schmidt, Carl - The Books Of Jeu And The Untitled Text In The Bruce Codex

Jacobs, Alan - The Essential Gnostic Gospels

Alcock, Anthony - A Coptic Magical Text. - Bulletin of the American Society of Papyrologists

Aune, David E. - Magic in Early Christianity

Benko, Stephen. "Early Christian Magical Practices." In Society of Biblical Literature, 1982 Seminar Papers

Betz, Hans Dieter, ed. The Greek Magical Papyri in Translation

Borghouts, J. F. Ancient Egyptian Magical Texts

The Magical Texts of Papyrus Leiden

Brier, Bob. Ancient Egyptian Magic

Crum, Walter E - Magical Texts in Coptic, Journal of Egyptian Archaeology

DuQuesne, Terence - A Coptic Initiatory Invocation

Gager, John G., ed - Curse Tablets and Binding Spells from the Ancient World

Griffith, FL - The Date of the Old Coptic Texts and Their Relation to Christian Coptics

The Old Coptic Magical Texts of Paris

The Leyden Papyrus: An Egyptian Magical Book

Preisendanz, Karl. - Deux papyrus magiques de Ia collection de Ia Fondation egyptologique

Ritner, Robert K. - The Mechanics of Ancient Egyptian Magical Practice

Worrell, William H. - Coptic Magical and Medical Texts

"A Coptic Wizard's Hoard." American Journal of Semitic Languages and Literatures

J.C.B. Petropoulos - GREEK MAGIC Ancient, Medieval and Modern

Mastrocinque, Attilio - From Jewish Magic to Gnosticism

Marvin Meyer - Magic and Ritual Power

Ancient Christian Magick; Coptic Texts of Ritual Power

MacDermot, Violet The Books of Jeu and the Untitled Text in the Bruce Codex

BIBLIOGRAPHY

PAPYRI

John Rylands University Library Papyrus Collection, The University of
Manchester, U.K
B 6749
B 2218
B 2892
B 5652
Coptic MS 103
Coptic MS 104

Bodleian Library, Codex Brucianus, Bruce 96

Duke University, Duke Papyrus Archive
P.Duk.inv. 231
P.Duk.inv. 256
P.Duk.inv. 475
P.Duk.inv. 811 R
P.Duk.inv. 645

Oxyrhychus Papyrii
Oxy.VI 0864
Oxy.XIII 1613
Oxy.VI 0886
Oxy.XVI 2061

Oxy.LXV 4468
Oxy.LVI 3834
Oxy.LXVIII 4674
Oxy.XXXVI 2753
Oxy.LXVIII 4673
Suppl.Mag.II 88
Suppl.Mag.II 56

www.ingramcontent.com/pod-product-compliance
Lightning Source LLC
Chambersburg PA
CBHW031121020726
47495CB00007B/2293